IRON
RIVER

12/2018

IRON RIVER

DANIEL ACOSTA

CINCO PUNTOS PRESS ⬥ EL PASO, TEXAS

An excerpt from *Iron River* was published in *Label Me Latino/a*, Fall 2016, Volume VI, page 8.

FIRST EDITION
10 9 8 7 6 5 4 3 2 1

Library of Congress Cataloging-in-Publication Data

Names: Acosta, Daniel (Teacher), author.
Title: Iron river / by Daniel Acosta.
Description: First edition. | El Paso, Texas : Cinco Puntos Press, [2018]
Summary: When twelve-year-old Manny Maldonado and his friends find a hobo's body near the train tracks that run through their tight-knit San Gabriel valley community, a police officer tries to pin the murder on them.
Identifiers: LCCN 2017057540 | ISBN 978-1-941026-93-9 (hardback : alk. paper) | ISBN 978-1-941026-94-6 (paper : alk. paper)
ISBN 978-1-941026-95-3 (e-book)
Subjects: | CYAC: Murder—Fiction. | Railroads—Fiction. | Friendship—Fiction. Police—Fiction. | Mexican Americans—Fiction. | Family life—California—Fiction. | California—History—20th century—Fiction.
Classification: LCC PZ7.1.A226 Ir 2018 | DDC [Fic]—dc23
LC record available at https://lccn.loc.gov/2017057540

Book and cover design by Bluepanda Studios

¡Gloria a Dios!

FOR LINDA
con amor y cariño

$$1$$

November 1958

I'm telling you this now because I don't know when I'm going to die. If you ask me why is a twelve-year-old kid thinking about dying, well, I don't want to die. You hear people say they wish the old people had wrote things down because now they're dead and their stories didn't get told. But sometimes people die who aren't old and that got me thinking: people don't always die when they think they're going to. So I want to tell you this story in case I die before I get old.

My friends call me "Man-on-Fire." My best friend Danny Valdez gave me that nickname. Danny said my port-wine stain and my red hair made me look like I'm on fire, and now everybody in Sangra calls me "Man-on-Fire." I'm red-headed and have light skin and blue eyes like my dad, and my port-wine stain starts under my left arm and goes across my neck and covers part of my jaw all the way to my right ear. It doesn't bother me anymore when people stare at my birthmark because I'm proud to have such a great nickname.

My real name's Manuel Maldonado, Junior. Except on my birth certificate, my name's spelled "M-a-n-e-u-l." My mom says the lady at the hospital wrote it down wrong. Mom saw the mistake and asked her to fix it and the lady said she would, but she never did. Mom says it's because we're Mexican and the lady didn't want to go to the trouble. On my baptism paper, the lady in the church office knew what she was doing and wrote my name correct.

I pay attention to people's names. Like Betty. Betty's my mom's sister and my favorite aunt. Her real name is Betulia, which is from the Bible, I hear, but she hates it and makes faces when Grandma calls her that.

Betty lives two blocks away on Sunset Avenue with Uncle Ted. In the summer, while Mom's at work, Grandma takes care of me, except she wants me out of the house after breakfast, and I can't go back in until lunchtime. She likes the house to herself, but she lets me ride my bike to Betty's. So when I get bored and none of my friends are around, I go visit Betty.

I never have to knock on her door or anything. I just go right in. She did tell me to use the back door and park my bike in the back yard so nobody steals it. Most of the kids in the neighborhood got their bikes stole from somebody else. Kids just steal them from each other and paint them. I bet some kids are riding their own bikes and don't even know it.

What I like about Betty is that she loves me like her own kid. I asked Mom if I could stay every day at Betty's while she was at work, but she told me she didn't want me bothering Betty and besides it would hurt Grandma's feelings. I was disappointed but I guess I understand.

I go over Betty's and look in her refrigerator and help myself to food anytime. She buys milk from Riverside Dairy. It tastes better than the Valley Fresh Grandma gets delivered. Riverside tastes like clover. I love the taste of clover. On hot summer days, I pull the clover from where it grows near the faucet in Grandma's garden, and I suck on the little stems. I used to drink Riverside milk and close my eyes and taste the sweet clover in it and imagine like I was sitting in the shade of a tree in a giant field of sweet clover until my cousin Cruz, who thinks he knows everything, told me dairy cows eat alfalfa and that's what gives the milk that taste.

I wish he hadn't said that. When I drink Riverside now I still taste clover, but I can't help thinking about stacked-up bales of alfalfa instead.

I especially like to go over to Betty's when it's hot. I can stay in the house and sit in her cool parlor while she cleans house. Betty calls her front room her parlor.

When I told Mom that's what Betty called it, she made a kind of snort like she didn't like the word.

Anyway, I like to sit in Betty's parlor and look at her fireplace. I haven't seen too many fireplaces, but I never saw a fireplace like Betty's. It has tiles that show fairytale scenes of people sitting by a river or in boats shaped like tree leaves. Some of the people are half-human and half-goat or horse or something. Some of them are sleeping and some are dancing and some are fishing or splashing in the river. My favorite is this one little guy with red hair like me. He's not wearing a shirt. From his butt down to his feet is like a goat. He's sitting on a tree root that's sticking up from the ground and he's playing a flute. When I get to high school, I want to learn how to play the saxophone. On a hot day looking at the people in the fireplace really cools me off.

Betty doesn't mind if I look around her house. She has a room she calls the nursery.

There's no baby in Betty's nursery. There's no crib or any other thing that would be in a nursery. Betty says that it'll be a real nursery when she has a baby. She says she's afraid if she calls the room something else she'll never have that baby.

I found Ted's Purple Heart in the nursery. It's in a glass case with a nice wood base. I never saw one before so I took it over to Betty who was cleaning her bathroom floor, and I asked her what it was. When she saw me holding the Purple Heart, her eyes got real big and scared-looking.

She got up from the floor and took it from me. She didn't seem mad at me. She just looked kind of scared. I followed her back to the nursery and watched her set it on the shelf like it was a holy thing. She turned around and got down to my eye level and put her hands on my shoulders. She talked soft and told me I could touch anything else in the house, but I should never touch the Purple Heart. Ted won it in the war. She laughed after she said *he won it*. I asked her why she laughed. She said it's an award nobody wants to win, but it's better than the other. I asked her what the other was, and she just shook her head and told me that I could look at it all I wanted, but I couldn't touch it. She also told me not to ask Ted about the Purple Heart or about the war. I promised her I would do what she said.

$$2$$

San Gabriel is ten miles east of Los Angeles. We have one of Junipero Serra's twenty-one famous Spanish missions. The old-timers named our Mexican neighborhood Sangra, which is short for San Gabriel. The rest of the city is pure white people.

But not all the people in Sangra are Mexicans. The Yamanakas are Japanese. My know-it-all cousin Cruz told me they used to live in the white part of San Gabriel but during the war they had to sell their house and go to some kind of camp for Japanese people. He told me the government was afraid they were spies or traitors so they moved them to camps in the middle of nowhere. When they came home after the war, the price to buy their house back was too high so they ended up in Sangra.

Kiko Yamanaka is twelve years old like me and she's about the prettiest girl I ever saw. She looks like those dolls they sell in Chinatown. Her skin is whiter than white people's and she has these tiny red lips that make her look like a China doll. But me and Kiko probably won't get married because she's Japanese and I'm Mexican.

Besides the Yamanakas, there was another family called the Collisons who are *negros*. I say *was* because they moved back to Texas after the murder. Mister Collison worked for the Southern Pacific and his daughter Melinda was in my class at school. She came to our school in fourth grade from Houston. Melinda's family isn't Catholic, but Mr. Collison talked the principal into letting Melinda go to our school because he wanted her to get a better education than the public school.

It was her brother Lawrence who was murdered.

Last year Melinda did her report on the Southern Pacific and she told the class all about the railroad. I think her dad helped her. I asked her for her notes when she was finished. I found out that the gravel under the rail ties is called the ballast shoulder and other good train stuff.

My report was on port-wine stains.

The SP goes past our house on Main Street and all the way through eight states till it ends at the Atlantic Ocean in the state of Georgia. I know this because the train station in Alhambra has this big map on a wall in the waiting room and the route is marked by a red line. That map at the station is the best map I ever saw. I went to the Alhambra station about five times to say goodbye to company from Arizona or Jalisco who came to visit. When everybody else was outside waving bye, I'd be standing in front of that map trying to make it stick in my head so I wouldn't forget.

What I like best about that map is the pictures of the different places where the train stops. Next to Los Angeles is a painting of palm trees and our very own San Gabriel Mission. There's a painting of cactuses next to Tucson in Arizona, but there's no painting in New Mexico. If I was from New Mexico and I saw that map, I'd be mad.

In Texas there's a painting of the Alamo. I know all about the Alamo because me and my friends went to the San Gabriel Theater and saw the movie with Fess Parker as Davy Crockett fighting the Mexicans. I love that movie. That General Santa Anna was a bad guy so I'm glad the Texans won.

Me and my best friend Danny Valdez like to play the Alamo next to the SP tracks on the stretch of ground they call the rightaway. In the summertime, weeds grow there, and it's covered in trash—mainly beer cans and bottles. But in the springtime, the grass grows so high you can hide in it. Later I'll tell you about a time me and Danny did a dare there, but right now I want to tell you about the Battle of the Alamo.

Danny lives with his mom and dad and grandma Doña Tí and his brothers Rafa and Món and his beautiful sister Sonia. Sonia would win for Mission Fiesta Queen or Miss San Gabriel every year except the girls in the Fiesta Court have to go to Mission Catholic High and Sonia goes to public high school. And she's Mexican. They always pick a white girl for Miss San Gabriel.

My cousin Cruz is Sonia's age and all he does is talk about her. All the Sangra guys talk *about* Sonia, but they're too chicken to talk *to* her. Not me. I talk to her all the time.

In summer when I go over Danny's to see if he wants to play, Sonia's usually sitting on her front porch in the shade. Her hair's still kind of wet and curly like she just took a bath. Some girls don't look pretty until after they put on their makeup, but Sonia is already beautiful without that stuff. Her skin is smooth and her eyes always sparkle when she says hi to me. She has these beautiful brown eyes the color of root beer. They're kind of like

Kiko's Japanese eyes—except she's Mexican. And she wears these short skirts that really show off her brown legs. Sonia has nice legs. They're smooth and shiny and the color of those butterscotch candies they sell at Silverman's Market.

When I go over to play with Danny, Sonia calls me up to their porch and gives me a big hug and tells me I'm the cutest boy in the neighborhood. When she squeezes me, her *chichis* press against my chest and make me lose my breath. And when she squeezes me, her curly hair smells like lemons and feels cool and wet on my cheek. And when I ask her if Danny's home she yells "Danny-come-outside-Manny-wants-you!" right in my ear. She always smiles and says, "Danny and Manny. You guys should be a singing group!" and then she lets me go.

Danny usually comes out after a minute, chewing on a taco. Beans and rice. He asks me if I want one, but I don't care for beans unless they have cheese. He finishes his taco then wipes his hands on his pants. We go to the back and get the Radio Flyer his *ninos* gave him one Christmas. We cross the street to the rightaway and fill the wagon with beer cans and bottles that didn't break when the people threw them out their car windows. Beer cans are okay, but we like to find bottles better because they break when we hit them with rocks. After the wagon is full, we spend a long time deciding where to put the Mexicans.

When we first started playing the Alamo, we couldn't decide if we wanted to be the Texans or the Mexicans. Me and Danny are Mexican. To be the Texans would feel like traitors. But the Texans in the movie won, and we didn't want to be losers.

Finally we decided to be the Texans because it was just the two of us, but there were at least thirty bottles and cans in the wagon—outnumbered just like the Texans. So we spent a long time setting up the Mexicans on the rightaway and on the tracks. We lined the cans up side by side on the rails like rows of Mexican troops.

Don't worry, beer cans can't derail a train. I know because we've put pennies and nails and big rocks and even chunks of wood on the tracks to see if we could derail one, but we never could.

At the San Gabriel Theater, they always put on this short movie called *Dangerous Playground* before the real movie starts. *Dangerous Playground* is about how dangerous it is to play on the tracks. The Sangra kids make fun of it. For one thing, the kids in the movie are white. I never saw a real white kid play on the tracks.

Second, those kids seem pretty dumb. They stick their feet in switch tracks and stuff like that. Everybody knows that's dangerous. You don't need a movie to tell you that. And we know the movie is really fake because when an engineer catches the kids playing in the train yard, he doesn't call the cops. If those kids were Mexicans, he would've called the cops and the kids and their parents would've gone to jail. That's what Cruz says. And he knows everything. At least that's what he thinks.

I don't know about you but to me throwing rocks is about the best thing a boy can do besides spitting from high places. I don't like to hock loogies as much as I like to let them just drop. Danny tells me there a place in France called the Eiffel Tower that's so tall that if you let a loogie drop, it takes like an hour for it to hit the ground.

I hope I get to go up that tower someday.

I don't get to high places much, but there's always rocks to throw if a boy just looks for them. And things to throw rocks at.

Anyway, we put the bottles here and there on the rightaway.

Some we hid behind big rocks and some behind clumps of weeds and a few we stood out in the open like easy targets. Then we filled the Flyer with rocks and pulled it back across the street.

After we killed a few Mexican bottle-officers and knocked over some can-soldiers, we got bored and decided to quit.

Next day not a single bottle-officer was left standing. We expected the cans on the rails to be gone because the trains kill them, but it seems the bottle-officers got killed when we weren't around, maybe at night.

Who knows? Maybe it's the Angel of Death. Last year in Bible History, Sister Francis Assisi told us about the Angel of Death and the Egyptians. I want to stay up all night some night and look out my window for the Angel of Death to fly by across the street killing bottle-officers with her rocks.

The Southern Pacific Railroad is like a river. Sometimes the current flows east when an engine pulls out of Los Angeles dragging a line of cars behind it. I call it a strong current when four big, loud locomotives are hitched in line and roar by pulling more than two hundred boxcars. Sometimes the cars are full and their side doors are shut and locked, but other times they run empty and the doors are wide open so you can try to throw rocks right through to the other side.

I say the current is light when a locomotive goes by pulling less than fifty cars. The current usually runs slower when the trains are heading west to Los Angeles. East currents usually carry empty boxcars.

When we aren't killing Mexicans, me and Danny and our friends Little and Marco throw rocks at trains. Little's favorites to throw at are the car-cars. The car-cars are double-deckers that carry brand new cars to Los Angeles. I don't think he should do that because who wants to buy a car with broken windows or scratched paint, but Little still does. He says his dad'll never buy a new car so what difference does it make.

Once I asked Danny if his brother Raul ever bought a new car. Raul is Danny's oldest brother if you don't count Joaquín who was killed in Korea. You probably heard of Raul Valdez. He pitches for the Chicago White Sox. All of Sangra is proud of him because he made it to the big leagues. When the Sox come to California for spring training, Raul spends most of his free time with his family. When he comes to San Gabriel, the whole city— even the white people—follows him around town. Danny says even though Raul has the money to sleep in fancy hotels, he likes to stay at home because he misses his family and there's no Mexican food as good as his mom's.

Danny said Raul bought a new T-Bird last summer, but he keeps it in Chicago where he lives.

In that movie *Dangerous Playground,* a little white girl riding the passenger train gets hurt when a boy throws a rock and breaks her window. But it's fake because that window glass is too thick to break with a little rock. Our rocks just bounce off them.

Twice a day three times a week, shiny locomotives pull passenger trains east and west. The east-current trains pass at around nine in the morning and the west around five in the afternoon. It's always fun to stand on the rightaway and wave to the people. It's always pure white people looking out the windows. Sometimes they wave back.

Melinda Collison's father is a porter on those trains.

Not all passengers ride the passenger trains on the SP. Summer or winter you can see bunches of hobos sitting or standing on top of boxcars on their way east or west. Where we live, there's a bend in the tracks that makes the trains have to slow down. That's good for us because it's easier to throw rocks at a slow train. Sometimes the train even stops for a long time when there's an accident up ahead. It can stand there for over an hour before it starts up again with a big jolt and the sound of four hundred couplers banging together.

It's when the train is stopped that the hobos come to Grandma's.

3

I used to run inside the house and hide in the front room when I saw a hobo coming. Soon there would be a soft knock on the door. Grandma would answer it and open the big door while I stood behind her. The hobos would hold their hats in their hands and they'd be real dirty because they get covered in the black smoke the locomotives blow out. Grandma would tell them to wash up at the faucet in the front yard while she went to make them something to eat.

I know not to unlatch the screen door. Grandma says that's her protection, but I can't see how a little metal hook can really stop a man if he wants to go inside.

The hobos eat Grandma's sandwiches sitting in what I call the hobo chair on her cool front porch. I've even seen some men say grace and bless their food before they ate.

Grandma usually makes them minced-ham sandwiches or *tacos de frijoles*. Some carry thermos bottles and Grandma washes them and fills them with coffee while they eat.

I used to wish I could sit down and talk to them while they were eating. You know, to hear about where they're going or where they've been and what life is like on the rails. But Grandma told me to leave them in peace. Don't disturb their dignity, she would say. So I settled for just watching them through the venetian blinds in my bedroom.

When they're finished, Grandma takes the dirty dish and cup—she always serves them on our dishes and cups. She gives them back their thermos filled with fresh coffee and a couple more sandwiches wrapped in wax paper. The men usually don't say much, but I heard one or two tell her, "God bless you, ma'am." After she closes the door she makes the sign of the Cross behind them to bless them on their way. When they get to the street mostly they run across and jump back on the train. But sometimes a hobo will kneel down and make some kind of sign in chalk or charcoal on the sidewalk in front of our house.

After what happened I don't go to the door anymore when hobos knock.

You already know my best friend Danny. Well, besides him, my other best friends are Marco and Little. Marco's whole name is Marco Antonio Julio César Rivas. He says his mom gave him that name because she thought it was in the Bible somewhere.

Sister Margaret Mercy—who Marco calls Margaret Murphy— told him his name isn't in the Bible, but that it comes from Roman history. Marco's the youngest kid in our gang. I'm almost a year older than him. He's about the smartest kid I know. He gets straight A's in school, and he loves to read. He has bookshelves stuffed with books in his front room. Other neighborhood kids tease him and tell him who does he think he is, white?

I hate that about Sangra. Whenever a person does something good or gets an award for something, they always say, "Who does he think he is?" or "He thinks he's all good." I hate it the most when they say, "Who does he think he is, white?" I think that's part of why my uncle Rudy went back to prison.

Marco lives at the corner of Main and California where the street makes an L right next to the train tracks. His bed is barely two feet from the rails. He says when the train goes by at night, his house shakes and his bed bucks like a rodeo bronco. The windows rattle so much that his mom stuffs rags tight around them so they won't break like all the windows on Main Street do. Marco says his mom tells his dad she's going to divorce him if they don't move.

Little's my last best friend. His real name is Carlos Gutierrez. I'll tell you about why we call him "Little" later because I need to tell you what happened that made me think I might die before I get old.

School was out for the summer, but it was a cool day because clouds were blocking the sun. Me and Danny and Little went over Marco's house to see what we could do. Marco was sitting on his front steps when we got there. Nobody said anything until Danny spoke up.

"Wanna go to the wash?" Little said.

Rubio Wash is a storm channel the other side of San Gabriel Boulevard. Cruz told me it starts at the San Gabriel Mountains in Pasadena. It comes south past our neighborhood then "flows" into the San Gabriel River at the Whittier Narrows. I say "flows" as a joke because there's usually just a little bit of water in it, which makes it easy to jump over. There are all kinds of things to find down there in the wash: old tires and shopping carts from the Safeway and wooden boards and broken toys and sometimes dead animals. We have to crawl through a long drainage pipe to get to the wash.

"Nah," Danny said, "I don't wanna get dirty."

"How about the hobo park?" I said. The hobo park is a clump of bushes and weeds up the tracks where hobos sometimes camp. We're not allowed to go there. If somebody from Sangra saw us there, they'd call up our mom or grandma and tell them we're up to no good. The neighborhood is like that. You can't do anything without people knowing who you are and who your family is and what you're up to.

Smith Park's the real city park. The pool opens the second week of summer, but it's usually too crowded until after Fourth of July. Plus, the teenage guys hog all the games in the rec room anyway.

I'm not ever allowed to go to Smith Park by myself at night. At night Smith Park is a dangerous place. That's where the tecatos hang out. Tecatos is what we call heroin addicts. Cruz calls them "tee-cats." I know about tee-cats because my uncle Rudy was one.

Betty doesn't like me to use that word to describe him.

We didn't plan what happened. One minute we heard the horn of the 9:40 freight train coming out of L.A. on an east current, and the next minute we were in Marco's backyard throwing oranges and lemons at the hobos riding on top of the boxcars. It was a light current, and before I knew it the caboose went by and the tracks were quiet again. We looked at each other kind of in shock because we never did that before—throw fruit at hobos.

"We better pick up the fruit before my mom comes out," Marco said. "If she finds out we did this, she's going to whip me. And then she's going to tell my dad when he gets home, and he's going to whip me too."

When we got to the tracks, the ballast shoulder was covered with smashed oranges and lemons. Wherever I looked was orange and yellow and green.

Marco said, "What are we going to do with all this stuff? We can't put it back on my trees."

We stood there quiet, thinking and thinking.

"I have an idea," Little said. "Let's take it to the pipe and dump it down the wash."

"There's too much to carry," I said.

Finally Danny said, "I'll go get my wagon, and we can load it up. It's big enough to hold all the fruit."

It took about ten minutes to get the smashed fruit into the wagon and drag it to the rightaway. Me and Little pushed and Danny and Marco pulled the Flyer.

That's when we saw what looked like a bundle of clothes. It was Little who first realized it was a body. We walked real slow to get close.

It was a man, a hobo. He was face down on the rightaway. Little pointed at one of the hobo's arms twisted behind his back in a way people can't put their arms. His right leg was in a wrong way under him and his foot was missing its shoe.

"His arm's broke nearly off," Little said.

Danny's eyes were filling with tears.

"What are we going to do?" I asked.

Little said, "We killed him."

Marco turned to Little. "One of us did."

"Who hit him?" I tried to remember every fruit I threw.

Little was serious. "If we don't know who did it, they'll put all of us in prison."

"Do they send little kids to prison?" Marco asked Little. Tears were rolling down his cheeks.

"Juvvie," said Little. "At least till we turn eighteen."

We stared at the body. I bit my thumbnail. It tasted like lemon. "Maybe we can take him to the wash."

It got real quiet. Even the cars stopped crossing the tracks. A crow on the telephone wires squawked over us, and we jumped. We all looked at the wagon loaded with smashed fruit. We would have to dump it to load in the smashed man.

"We need to call the cops," Marco said real quiet. He was right. "I'll be back. Wait for me and don't touch him."

I told Little and Danny, "I didn't really mean I wanted to dump him in the wash."

"I knew you wouldn't do that when it came down to it," Little said.

I looked down at the dead man again. He was wearing farmer's overalls and a jacket that goes to a suit. The hand of his broken arm was the color of ashes. His hair was brown and gray in places and greasy-looking. The foot that had a shoe was wearing a worn-out brown boot.

"¡Ay, Dios mío! What did you boys do now?"

I turned and saw Marco walking toward us with his mom at his side. She was wearing a flowery yellow apron that didn't go with her dark green dress, and she was wiping her hands on the bottom of the apron. Her face was all pulled together. When we got out of the way and she saw the hobo's body, she stopped cold like she walked into a wall. She covered her mouth with her hands. She looked at the wagon and the smashed fruit.

None of us answered.

"I called the police, and they will be here soon. Did you touch it?"

"No," Danny answered. His tear tracks were clean streaks down his dusty face.

I expected to hear a bunch of sirens, but only one police car drove up on the rightaway from San Gabriel Boulevard. It started coming toward us. The car stopped in back of the hobo's body and a cloud of dust blew over him. After a long time, the driver's door opened and a policeman climbed out slow.

My heart sank to my stomach. His last name is Turkness, but Sangra calls him *Turco*. The Turk. We knew that he had it in for Mexicans so steer clear of him. He did whatever he wanted to whoever he wanted and got away with it.

The Turk stood with his hands on his gun belt and looked down at the hobo, then over at us. He was squinting in the dusty light. He went to his car and came back wearing his hat and sunglasses. He looked even scarier with the glasses on. He turned his head without moving his neck like owls do. I knew he was looking at the wagon full of smashed fruit.

He walked over to the body and squatted down. He lifted the hobo's shoulder, tipping the body so he could see underneath. He let it drop back down. Without standing up or looking at us, he said, "What happened here?"

We stood quiet.

"I said, what happened here?" The Turk's voice was deeper than my dad's and echoed inside itself.

"We were throwing fruits at the train," Little answered.

"That's against the law. You boys should know that." We knew.

The Turk got up and stood staring at us for a long time. I wanted him to hurry so whatever punishment was coming would come fast, and we could get it over with. He turned and walked back to his car and pulled out the radio handset. He looked at us when he talked into the radio. There was loud static and a voice over the radio said something. The Turk hung up and came back to us holding a sheet of paper.

"Are you their mother?" he asked Mrs. Rivas. She pulled Marco so his back was against her and she put her arms over his chest.

"Only this one is mine."

The Turk turned to me.

"You speak English?"

"Yes, sir."

He turned his head to Little.

"You?"

"Yes, Officer."

"All you boys read and write English?"

We nodded without saying anything. He handed the paper to Mrs. Rivas.

"Where do you live?"

Mrs. Rivas pointed to her house. We turned to see her backyard. Her fruit trees were naked.

"Take the boys to your house and have them fill out that sheet. Names and addresses." He pointed at the paper. "When the meat wagon gets here, I'll come for it."

Mrs. Rivas steered Marco toward their house. Danny and Little and me followed.

♐

I had to stay in the front room the rest of the day. Grandma wouldn't let me watch television. She said she'd talk to my dad when he got home and to stay put until he did. Then finally I could get punished—and that would be that—until the cops came for me.

My mind wouldn't slow down. Everything that happened that morning ran through my brain a hundred miles an hour, like a freight train on a fast current.

I tried to think about other things. I listened to my Grandma in the kitchen cleaning the supper beans. I heard them rattle into the metal pot on the seat of the kitchen chair when she swept them off the table with her hand. They made a sound like the rocks we dropped into the Flyer. Now I could hear the big pot bubbling on the stove.

I was staring out the screen door when Dad's car pulled into the driveway. In a minute, I heard Mom and Dad talking to Grandma. It was all too low for me to understand. All I could hear was the rumble of Dad's voice. That rumbly voice usually meant trouble.

I was still staring out the screen door when I felt my dad's strong hand on my shoulder. He turned me around. He was squatting down like the Turk. I was eye to eye with him. His blue eyes shined with the light coming through the screen door. The whites of his eyes were streaked with red. They looked tired and sad.

"What happened, son?"

Jeez, I did pretty good not to cry all day like Danny and Marco. But now in front of my dad—seeing his look—I just couldn't hold it back anymore. My eyes blew up. My tears burned. I wrapped my arms around my dad's neck and pressed my face against his. I didn't care if his cheek scraped my face and made it sting.

"I'm sorry, Daddy." My heart wanted to break in half.

He put his arms around me and pulled away from me—real slow—so he could see my face.

"Just tell me what happened."

It was past supper by the time I finished telling Dad about the fruit and the hobo and the Turk. Grandma kept our dinner hot. Me and Dad ate in the kitchen alone. We didn't talk.

After supper I sat by myself in the bedroom I shared with Cruz, going over and over what happened on the rightaway. I never saw a dead person before except Grandpa in his coffin.

Grandma knocked on the door and told me to come to her room and pray the rosary with her for the intention of the dead hobo. Grandma prays the rosary every night at eight o'clock. It comes on the radio in Spanish. Some priest says the *Dios Te Salve, Marías*, and a group of old Mexican ladies say the *Santa Marías*. I usually do everything I can to get out of praying the rosary, but this time I thought I better.

When I got to her room, Grandma was already kneeling next to her bed with her crystal rosary in her wrinkly hands. I kneeled next to her. She handed me the rosary with black beads that used to belong to Grandpa. I don't think he used it much because it was still pretty shiny and new looking. The crystal beads of Grandma's were dull. Even the silver links between the beads were black and dull from being used over and over again.

Next to Grandma's bed on top of her dresser is a big glass case where she keeps her *santos*. There must be fifty statues of different saints and a few of Baby Jesus in rich costumes like the *Santo Niño de Atocha*. Her favorite saint is Martin of Tours. She has a picture of him on the wall next to the saints' case and one on the kitchen calendar from *La Princesa* Market.

Martin of Tours is a Roman soldier sitting on a horse. In front of him is an old man sitting on the ground naked except for a white towel covering his you-know-what. In the picture, Saint Martin is cutting his red cape in half with his sword.

At the front of the case, there's a small statue of Saint Sebastian tied to a tree with arrows sticking out of him. I'm not too crazy about Sebastian because the statue has kind of a girl's face and Sebastian is standing all like a girl, with his hands tied up over his head. I don't bother praying to him because I figure he knows how I feel about him.

My favorite is St. Bartholomew. He's bigger than Sebastian and tied up to a tree too, but big strips of his skin are missing from his chest and legs. You can see the red meat in those spots. One time I asked Sister Francis Assisi why he looked that way and she told me the pagans flayed him: they peeled his skin off while he was still alive.

I prayed the rosary a million times before with Grandma.

Sometimes it's easy to think about the prayers and pray real hard, like when Grandpa was in the hospital with his stroke so he would get well. Other times I think about everything else but the *Padre Nuestros* and *Diós Te Salve Marías*. I think about

Cruz watching TV in the front room and my little sister Dorothy playing with her dolls and why don't Cruz and Dorothy have to pray too? Those are the times I look at each *santo* and ask them to tell God not to be mad at me for thinking about every other thing besides him.

I'm an altar boy at the San Gabriel Mission. Once in awhile, I think about dying for my faith. And once in a while I think about what I'd do if a communist barged into the church during Mass and aimed a gun at Father Simon when he's holding up the bread or wine. I'd see the gun and jump up just in time to take the bullet meant for Father Simon. That would get me straight into heaven and it wouldn't hurt as much as being flayed.

Like I said, some nights I have a heck of a time praying, but that night the prayers came hot and heavy. I prayed for the poor hobo and wondered what sins he committed in his life. If he stole anything, I'm sure God would forgive him because he was poor. So I prayed that God would let him into heaven. And if he had to go to Purgatory first, I asked God to let him slide and I would suffer for him since I was the one who put him there in the first place.

But if I have to suffer, don't make me be flayed.

Cruz is probably going to blab on me anyway so I might as well tell you now that I still wet my bed. I had to start sharing a room with him two years ago. Cruz' dad Lalo is Mom and Betty's brother, but Lalo's a mean drunk so we don't have much to do with him if we can help it. When he beat up Cruz one time too much and too bad, Grandma took Cruz in, and he's slept here ever since.

Anyway, every morning I wake up and the sheets are wet and cold and make the whole room stink of pee. I don't know why I still wet my bed. Mom and Dad took me to the doctor. When I told him I shared the bed with Cruz, the doctor asked me if Cruz ever tried to do anything nasty to me. I got embarrassed from that question and tried to remember if he ever did, but all I could come up with was the times he punched my arm when I said something stupid.

The doctor told us there didn't seem to be anything wrong with me and that I would stop sometime. So I sleep with a rubber sheet under my regular sheet. Every morning I have to shower off the smell of pee and take the sheets out to the washing machine in Grandma's *cuartito* behind the garage.

I don't know if it's the dream that makes me pee or the pee that makes me have the dream, but the dream's always the same. I'm sitting on Grandma's porch in the hobo chair when I hear the train horn extra-loud. I look toward Marco's house where the roar of the train is coming from. I wonder what train it is because it's not on schedule.

Then I see the engine roar past Marco's coming west way too fast. And that big black engine blowing black smoke over its head like it's mad at the world. I know it's going too fast to make the curve but I can't do anything but watch. And it's tilting over. I can see the wheels on the other side lifting off the tracks.

As soon as it passes Marco's, the engine falls on its side on the rightaway and then starts skidding on the street. Sparks fly into the sky and the train crushes Marco's house and comes sliding along Main Street towards me. The flying sparks turn into hobos getting thrown around like pieces of torn-up paper. The black train is swallowing houses like a huge, hungry black snake.

When it eats Danny's house, I scream but my voice gets drowned out by the train's horn. The big oak tree in front of Danny's explodes in a million burning leaves and the engine skids toward me. I try to get up and run but I can't move, like I'm glued to the hobo chair. I squeeze my eyes closed, trying to block out the engine's headlight and brace myself for the locomotive. I don't feel the engine slam into me. Just rough shaking. And all I can hear is the clickety-clack-clickety-clack of the cars when they cross the rail joints. I feel my blood oozing hot down my legs as I'm laying there on Grandma's porch dying.

"Get up, Pee Baby!" Cruz shakes me awake, pulls the rags away from the window, and opens it to get in some fresh air. "You pissed the sheets again." You'd think he'd get tired of saying the same thing every time, but he doesn't. I turn away from the light and cover my head with the blanket. Right away I smell my pee. My legs feel cold and clammy. When I turn, my hand touches the wet bottom sheet. I uncover myself and sit up. I wonder if I'm ever going to stop wetting the bed. Or having the train dreams.

"You gotta stop pissing the bed, man. I'm sick of it." When he says "man," he doesn't mean my nickname.

I get up and take off my pajamas and underwear. I don't care if I'm naked and Cruz is there. I just want to get the smelly clothes off. I strip the sheets and blankets off the bed and drop them in a pile on the floor. Then I put on my bathrobe and throw my underwear and pajamas on the pile. I carry the bundle out to the cuartito and drop it next to Grandma's washing machine. I wet the bed so much my mom had to buy three sets of sheets for me.

Mom and Dad were already gone to work, and Cruz took off after breakfast, but Grandma made it clear I had to stay in the yard the rest of the day. I got dressed, went out to the front porch, and waited for the police to come get me.

From the front porch, I can look past the tracks and the

warehouses with the broken windows and see the San Gabriel Mountains. Up on Mount Wilson, there's a place that looks just like a heart with an arrow sticking through it. I was sitting in the hobo chair just thinking about how smart God was to make that happen when Danny opened the gate and came into the yard.

"Hi, Man. What're you doing?" He seemed like his usual happy self. I wondered how come he wasn't worried like me.

"Nothing. Grounded. You?" I got up from the hobo chair. "Aren't you grounded too?"

Danny hopped on the low wall of the porch and started hitting his heels against the cement to the beat of a song he must've had in his head. He stopped kicking the wall. "Block-grounded. I can go as far as the corners. How far can you go?"

I pointed to the gate.

Danny stood up and rubbed his butt like he just remembered he had one. "I got a good whipping last night. It hurt like hell but at least that's over." Danny says hell like *hey-yell*. "I've got the block till the cops come get us. What do you think they're going to do to us?"

I didn't care about his sore butt. I was thinking the same thing about the cops. I didn't want to talk about it though.

I pointed to the heart with the arrow through it. "See that?"

"What?"

"The heart. It has an arrow going right through it."

Danny stared at the mountain for a long time. "Nah. I don't see anything."

"Never mind," I told him. "Let's go up to the club."

Last year Little found a shipping pallet in the alley behind Silverman's Market. We dragged it up to the roof of the little house my grandpa built in the back yard that Grandma rents to a couple who just came from Mexico and don't speak English. His name is Germán. It looks like "Ger-man" like the country but he says it like *hair-mon.* Her name is Yoci. All my cousin Cruz talks about is how big her *chichis* are.

Before they moved in, the house was empty for a long time so we dragged that pallet up to the roof along with a flat cardboard refrigerator box we found on the rightaway. A big avocado tree grows next to the garage and spreads like a tent over the little house. We climb the rusty fence to get to the tree to get to the roof where we hang around and be a club.

What I love about the club is that up there all my worries go away. I can just lay down on my back on the cardboard and stare up at the green leaves and avocados and squint when the wind moves them out of the way and the sun hits my eyes. It's cool up there and almost quiet. Sometimes I even fall asleep until Grandma calls me to wash up for supper.

I laid down on the cardboard and Danny laid down next to me so close I could feel the heat from his body. "Scoot over," I told him and he did. They say prison cells are real small and they pack prisoners in them like rats in a cage.

We both laid there quiet in the shade. I watched a jet airliner through a hole in the avocado tent cross the sky and leave two white lines behind it. I imagined I was on that plane flying away to where the cops couldn't find me.

"Man, I'm scared," Danny said. I didn't look at him. I didn't answer him. I must've fell asleep because I jumped when I heard the sound of somone on the rusty fence. Little looked like a big rat when he jumped from the fence to the tree to the roof.

Like rats in a cage.

I sat up and pulled my knees to my chest to make room for

him on the cardboard. I could see Little was as scared as me and Danny. I asked him, "Did the cops come to your house yet?"

"Would I be here if they did?" He shook his head. "I got a whipping when my dad got home from work. Then my mom grounded me to the yard, but I'm not going to sit there and wait for the *chotas* to come get me. They're going to have to find me first."

I thought about that. That sounded like a good idea.

"Is Marco coming?" I asked Little.

He wiggled his shoulders. "I don't know. He should. We should go down together."

Danny's look told me he agreed. We would sit up in the club until Marco came and the cops found us. But it didn't feel good. I felt like a trapped rat. And when I thought about the dead hobo, my heart felt like it had an arrow stuck through it and it hurt like hell.

$$5$$

Marco didn't come all day and neither did the police. When, even from up in the club, we could hear Grandma cleaning the beans in the kitchen, me and Little and Danny made our secret club handshake and climbed down to go home.

"*¿Dónde 'stabas?*" Grandma asked when I came in. "You were supposed to stay in the yard."

"I didn't go anyplace. I was up in the club."

She looked hard at me for a long time. Then she went back to her beans.

"*No molestes a Yoci.* They're good renters, and I don't want no complaints. Go wash up and wait in the *salón* for supper." That's what Grandma calls the front room.

My little sister Dorothy was playing with her dolls and watching the Mickey Mouse Club. I only like watching that show when they have something good on like *Davy Crockett* or *Elfego Baca* or *Spin and Marty*.

I barely sat down on the couch when I heard the *pachuco*

whistle through the screen door. A *pachuco* whistle is different than any other kind. It's three notes with the middle one higher than the other two. I heard it again and looked outside. Somebody was at the gate. I looked back at the kitchen. Grandma was busy in there. I heard the whistle again. I got up and went to the screen door. It couldn't be the police here to get me. I don't think they give the *pachuco* whistle when they come to arrest people. And hobos knock on the door.

It was one of the tecatos. His name's Marcel and he's cousins with our next-door neighbor Elvira. I know he's a tee-cat because I hear people talk about how he brings shame to his family. I didn't want to talk to him, but I thought if I didn't he wouldn't go away.

"Ey, Little Man," he said when I got down to the gate. *Liddo*. That's how he said *little*. "Is your tío here?" I didn't know what he was talking about. "Come on, Little Man. Rudy." He rolled the R in Uncle Rudy's name and said it like *Rrru-thee*.

I was still confused. Rudy was in Folsom. All of Sangra knew that.

"He's in...he's not home."

Marcel looked at me and smiled. "Well, when he gets here, tell him Lino dropped by." Marcel put his hands in his pockets, turned, and walked down the sidewalk. I thought he was going to go in Elvira's house, but he went past it and disappeared around the corner.

Lino? Must be short for Marcelino. I guess his name was Marcelino, but I always thought his name was Marcel. I went back inside and waited for Mom and Dad to get home from work. I missed lunch and I was starving.

♐

A week went by. Each day my heart jumped less and less in my chest when the phone or the doorbell rang or somebody knocked on the screen door. The cops probably had to check for our fingerprints and collect evidence, and that was going to take time.

I didn't see much of the gang. They were probably laying low like me. I wasn't grounded anymore, but I was afraid to leave the yard. When I saw the Turk go by on patrol, I made sure he didn't see me. It was a long week.

One night while I was watching TV, I heard Dad and Mom and Grandma in the kitchen talking in Spanish. They never do that unless something big happened. The last time they talked like that was when a little girl fell down a well in San Marino. Men worked for days to rescue her, but she was dead when they finally got her out. San Marino got famous all over the world. There were stories about Kathy Fiscus every day for a month in the *Herald Express*. It even came out on TV.

Anyway, I could hear from the way they were talking that whatever it was, was something big. When they were finished, my dad took me outside to the front porch. He sat on the hobo chair and I sat on the arm.

I was scared the police had told him they were coming for me or that him and Mom were getting a divorce. The last time we sat like this he told me my grandpa died in the hospital. That was two years ago. Now he was looking at me and the blue of his eyes looked cold and hard as ice.

"Son, I got a letter today. The prison board approved your

uncle Rudy for parole. He's getting out and coming home in a few days."

Right away I thought about that *tecato* Lino with the *pachuco* whistle.

My dad confused me. The news seemed good, but his eyes and voice told me it wasn't.

"Rudy's trouble. You know he's been in prison most of your life. Now he's coming to stay with us until he can find a job and get his own place. While he's here, you're going to have to sleep on the couch and Cruz is going to have to go home and live with his folks. I hope Rudy doesn't stay long. I don't want him here."

"But he's your brother." He didn't answer me. It was like he never even heard me.

"When he gets here, I want you to steer clear of him, *¿M'entiendes*? He's bad news. I want you to promise me." I nodded. "*¿Entiendes*?" I nodded again.

Even when I pestered her, Grandma never told me much about Uncle Rudy. Like it hurt her just to talk about him.

It was Cruz who gave me the story—how Rudy brought disgrace and shame to the family.

Rudy is Dad's younger brother. Cruz told me Rudy went to prison before I was born but was out for about six months when I was around five. I don't remember him because my dad wouldn't let him live with us even though Grandpa and Grandma wanted him to, so he stayed with Ted and Betty. Like I said, he was out for six months. Then he got caught using heroin, and they sent him back to prison. Nobody in the family ever went to visit him. I don't know why. If he was my son or brother, I would have.

Cruz said Rudy got kicked out of Mission High when he was a freshman. Then he went to public high school, but he made trouble so they kicked him out of there. He got picked up for shoplifting and smoking marijuana.

I asked Cruz if he ever smoked marijuana, but he told me to mind my own business.

When Rudy went to court, the judge told him he could choose between going to jail or joining the service. Rudy picked the service. Grandma said Rudy liked the service and was a good soldier. She said he fought in the war against the Germans in North Africa and Italy. He wasn't wounded and didn't get a Purple Heart like Ted, but Cruz says when Rudy came home he was different. Messed up in the head. Mad all the time.

At first he spent a month just sleeping and laying around the house. After, he started looking for a job, but pretty soon he was staying out late at night and leaving the house later and later in the day. Then he stopped looking for work at all. Grandpa was patient with him for a while. Grandpa even took Rudy to work with him, but then Rudy quit doing that too.

Cruz told me that at somebody's wedding Rudy got drunk and got into a fight with my dad. Grandpa had to break them up. Rudy got back into heroin and Cruz saw him with the tecatos once or twice at the Smith Park and in the alley behind Silverman's Market. Finally Rudy and some other guys got arrested and put on trial. Rudy went to prison and that's about it. I didn't know what he looked like because the only pictures we had of him were when he was little, but I guess I would recognize him if I saw him because he would probably look like my dad. Maybe he would look like me.

"What did you do today?"

My dad's question woke me up from the daydream. I got up and stretched. Then I sat down on the porch wall.

"Nothing."

It's funny because I always say *nothing* even if I played on the tracks or went to the show with the gang or crawled down into the wash. Or killed a hobo. "Nothing," I said again. But it was true this time. I was afraid to do anything.

"Why do you think you still wet your bed?" His question surprised me. I shrugged my shoulders, but I could feel my face getting hot. I got the feeling Dad wanted to talk to me. I could tell the Rudy news shook him up. And the news that I killed a hobo. He wanted to talk to me but he didn't know how.

"Do you want to hear a story about when I was a kid?" he said.

I did. Anything except about me wetting the bed. He leaned down in the hobo chair and turned so that the back of his head was facing me. He opened up his hair with his fingers so I could see the skin. He said, "Look at this." I barely saw a line whiter that the skin around it—like a jet plane trail in the sky.

"When I was a little kid on the ranch back in Arizona, I was sitting on a burro out in the corral. I had my arms and my legs crossed and I was balanced on the burro's rump, nice and fancy. Well, Rudy came up *detrás de mí* so I didn't see him. He must've pulled some hair from the burro's rump because that burro bucked one time, and I flew up in the air. When I hit the ground—and it was hard ground, all rocks—I still had my arms and legs *cruzados*. Can you picture that? I landed on my head and it split open like a *sandía*."

I wanted to cry because I was laughing so hard at the picture of Dad's head looking like a cracked-open watermelon.

"Well, not like a real sandía, but the skin split open and blood was gushing out. Rudy ran inside yelling for my 'amá. She came out and when she saw me, she screamed. She thought I was dead, but Rudy said I was just faking. But I wasn't. My face was covered in blood and I had a splitting headache." Dad laughed about the splitting part.

"When your grandpa got home and Grandma told him what happened and that Rudy wouldn't fess up to doing it, he marched him out to the yard and told him to drop his pants. He whipped him with a branch from the palo verde next to the outhouse. I think that hurt him more than my head hurt me!"

We laughed together and then he hugged me tight before we went inside. Later, when I was in bed, and Mom already said bedtime prayers with me, and Grandma blessed me a million times and tucked me in, Dad came to my room and looked down at me.

"Promise me you'll stay away from Rudy."

I nodded again. Then he blessed the sign of the Cross on my forehead with his rough thumb and kissed it and went out, closing the door behind him.

The next day, I was in my room moving my stuff from the chester drawers into a cardboard box. Cruz' drawers were empty because he was already moved back in with his folks on Pearl Street. I just finished putting my last shirt in the box, when I heard meowing out my front window. Danny. That was his secret signal. He read in *Huckleberry Finn* how Tom Sawyer or somebody used it as their gang's secret signal.

I started reading that book, but it was too hard because there's a bunch of spelling mistakes in it. Plus, when I tried to read the words that *negro* named Jim said, I couldn't understand any of it.

Danny says it's a great book and it probably is, but I have other things to do and too much to think about right now to try reading it again. I went to the window and pressed my face to the screen to make my nose go all flat like a boxer's.

"*Órale.*" Danny was trying to sound like a *pachuco*. I laughed. He went around to the screen door, and I let him in. He followed me back to my ex-room. He looked at the box with my clothes in it and the open chester drawers. "Are you going someplace, Man?" he asked me, all worried. "Did the cops come or something?"

"*Chale.*" I laughed. "Nah, my uncle Rudy's getting out of prison. Grandma's giving him my room for a while. I'm sleeping on the couch."

Danny smiled and watched me finish packing. When I was done he helped me carry the box to the corner of the front room next to the gas heater. I was going to put the box down when he stopped me.

"Not so close. It might catch on fire," he said.

We moved it next to the TV by the front window. I looked at him to see if this was okay, and he smiled. We put the box down.

"Why you smiling so much?"

He reached in his pocket and pulled out two dimes. "All we need is four more cents and we can get Cokes." I never have Cokes. The only thing I get to drink is Kool-Aid unless it's a big party or Christmas.

"Where did you get the dimes?" I asked him when he handed one to me.

"My *tío* came to visit and gave me them."

Danny followed me to the kitchen where Grandma was taking beans out of a big brown bag with an old coffee cup and spreading them on the kitchen table. It was strange for her to start cleaning beans this early, but I just stood there not saying anything until she turned, put her hand on her hip backwards the way women do, and looked at me.

"What do you want?" she asked.

"Nothing," I said. "Can I look for change in the *trastero*?"

Grandma nodded her head. I opened the trastero drawer where she keeps odds and ends. A trastero, in case you don't know, is the cabinet where you keep dishes and cups. I pushed around rubber bands and pencils with broken points and an ink pen that doesn't work and some small nails to hang pictures with and an old pair of my grandpa's glasses and some business cards and holy cards from the funerals of people from the neighborhood, and I found six pennies. I left two of them for the future and slammed the drawer shut.

"Can I go to Silverman's with Danny?"

Grandma looked over at him. I could see that he was trying to be all cute for her.

"As long as you stay out of trouble. I don't want nobody to call me on the phone telling me you were being *traviesos*."

I gave two pennies to Danny and put the other two in my pocket. We went out the side door headed for our Cokes at Silverman"s.

6

There's three little *marquetas* in Sangra: Silverman's Market and *La Princesa*—which Sangra calls *"Pendejadas"* because that's all they sell—and Tanaka's, but Mom buys her groceries up at Safeway because Ted works in the meat department. And besides, she says, Silverman cheats customers and Tanaka's is filthy.

I know what she means about Tanaka's. I only been in there a couple of times and that was just to see Tanaka's finger or show it to another kid.

Danny's brother Rafa told us about the finger. The story goes Tanaka chopped his pointer finger off one day cutting a piece of meat for a customer. He didn't go to the hospital, just put the finger back on the knuckle and wrapped a band-aid around it. The finger grew back except he put it on crooked so the fingernail is sideways.

I had to see it for myself so me and Danny went to Tanaka's one day to look. We went in and walked around so Tanaka wouldn't think we were there just to see his finger. That place was as dirty as I heard. There were dead flies on the sills of the front windows and spider webs in the top corners. There was a layer of dust on the cans and boxes. Can labels were faded and some were peeling off.

Tanaka keeps his candy in a big glass case to stop kids from shoplifting it. Danny pointed at the penny candies and held up two fingers in a V. Tanaka reached into the glass case, and I saw it, just like something in a museum. There was Tanaka's finger with the sideways fingernail! The thick glass made the finger look even bigger than real life. The pointer-finger looked normal and the color of a Tootsie Roll till about halfway up where it was almost black, and there on the side was Tanaka's fingernail all dark, ashy gray and cracked like an Egyptian mummy in its own glass case.

Out of the corner of my eye I saw Danny nod to Tanaka, and the old man grabbed two strips of button candies and held them out to us over the counter.

"Two cent," he said.

When we got outside, Danny threw the button candies down a storm drain.

The back of Silverman's Market is at the end of the alley on Sunset Avenue. What Mom said about Silverman's is true. Little told me Big told him. Big works at Silverman's. He's Little's half-brother.

There are two Gutierrez families in Sangra. Little Guti's family lives three blocks away from us on El Monte Street and Big Guti's family lives on Sunset Avenue next door to Ted and Betty and across from Silverman's. Big is three years older than Little and he goes to Mission High like Cruz. Both Gutis are named Carlos after their dad. They have the same number of brothers and sisters and—you won't believe this—they all have the same names too. I mean Big has a brother named Anthony and so does Little. And Big has three sisters named Marta and Irene and Stella. So does Little. And so we just call the two Carloses Big and Little to make it easier and to keep them straight.

When I found this out about the Gutierrez families, I asked Grandma if she knew more about them. She said that Carlos Gutierrez—the father—was married to the woman who lives on Sunset Avenue, but then he met the other woman, moved her into the house on El Monte Street, and they started living together. I know that's a sin, but they don't go to church except for Little so I guess it doesn't matter to them. Anyway, Missus Guti complained that he was married to her, so all three decided that they would share him fifty-fifty as long as he paid all the bills.

I told Grandma I thought that was a strange story, and she said at first she thought so too. But that was a long time ago, and Sangra didn't care anymore.

Big's job is to sweep Sid Silverman's floors and refill the shelves and help *viejitas* with their shopping bags and stop people from shoplifting. Big says people shop Silverman's when they don't want to walk all the way to Safeway, or they're short on grocery money for the week.

If they want eggs or a can of lard or flour for tortillas but don't have the money, Sid gives it to them and writes it down in little books called tabs. On payday the people pay their tabs. But Sid doesn't just write down what things cost. If a can of lard costs 60¢, he writes 64¢ on the tab. So when people come in to pay their tab, the higher price covers the shoplifting. That's Sid's story.

Customers steal from him because he cheats them. That's Sangra's story.

So when me and Danny walked into Silverman's, Sid stopped us at the front counter.

"What do you want?" He looked down at us like we were Mickey Cohen or something.

Danny told him, "We just want to buy a Coke, sir."

"Let me see your money," Sid said. We pulled out our coins and showed them to him.

Sid yelled "Carlos!" without taking his eyes off us, and then he reached for the telephone.

We looked at each other. We were done for. He was calling the cops and Big was going to hold us till the cops came. Grandma warned me not to get into trouble. I thought about her and Mom and Dad all in like two seconds flat. When Big got to the counter, Sid talked without looking at him. "I gotta make a call. Take these two to the back and make sure all's they get is two sodas."

Big was wearing a work apron and holding a broom. He jerked his head to tell us to follow him. The soda box was in the back near the meat counter. Big opened the lid and we stuck our hands into the ice water.

"I heard about the hobo," Big said. We kept our mouths shut. "Cruz told me."

Stupid Cruz, I thought. Thanks to him probably all of Sangra knew.

"I heard the Turk collared you." We didn't answer him.

We fished around in the ice water till our hands hurt, but all we pulled up were Nesbitt's and Dad's Root Beer bottles. Danny looked up at Big. "Aren't there any Cokes?"

Big looked down at the underwater bottle caps. "Not cold, I guess. I'll go get two from the back."

"I don't want a hot Coke," I told him.

"Me neither," Danny said.

I reached down and pulled out a Dad's and Danny grabbed a Nesbitt's strawberry. We paid Sid and took the alley behind Silverman's to get home.

On the way home, I was pretty quiet.

"What's the matter, Man?"

I took a drink from my Dad's. I didn't have an answer.

Danny said, "Is it the hobo or the cops? For me, it's the hobo."

Our shoes crunched along the dirt part of the alley. I took another sip of my soda. Danny kept talking.

"It didn't seem like killing the hobo was a big deal to the Turk, but I can't get him out of my head, seeing him all broken up in the dirt like that. Murder's a sin, Man. I don't want to go to hey-yell." He was right about all those three things: the Turk was like people say he is, and murder is a sin, and I didn't want to go to hell either.

I asked Danny, "Should we go to confession on Saturday?"

He already had that red smile you get when you drink Nesbitt's strawberry. He wiped his mouth with his arm, but the smile was still there. "Yeah, probably. Do you think the hobo's in hey-yell?"

Grandma always blesses the hobos. And me and Grandma prayed the rosary for him.

"I don't think so. Maybe Purgatory. I don't know. I hope not."

Danny was quiet this time. Then he said, "It's a hard life living like a hobo, don't you think? Always begging for food and people telling you to go away and even getting hurt. Rafa told me those railroad cops they call bulls beat up hobos real bad."

We were about halfway down the alley where the ground was like street and our steps got quiet.

Danny said, "Sometimes when the train goes by, and I see them sitting on top of the boxcars, I wonder what it's like to travel all over the place and see different things. Different places and different people, even if you have to beg off them or get beat up."

That's one reason Danny's my best friend: because I was thinking the exact same thing. Another reason is that I can trust him with any secret I have, like wetting my bed.

We kept walking.

"Hey, remember the time we did the dare thing at the tracks? Did you get scared?" Danny asked me.

"Hell yeah!"

"Me too!" And we laughed.

I thought back to that day in April when the spring grass was as high as my belt on the rightaway, and we could cut trails in it and lay down in it and suck on its sweet roots.

I don't remember who dared who to get closest to the train, but we laid in the tall grass waiting, and when the engine passed we crawled through the grass till we got to the edge of the ballast shoulder.

We started to crawl on our stomachs like crabs, sideways, little by little toward the rails, facing each other. At first I was closer, then Danny got closer. I crawled until the next thing I knew my hair was being pulled up by the wind of the train. Then I felt my body being pulled up too. I looked over and saw the shiny rims of the steel wheels flashing by real close. The clicking wheels crossing the rail joints were so loud I couldn't hear my heart pounding, but I could feel it. I thought the train was going to pull me in. I grabbed any part of the ballast shoulder I could to make myself stick to the ground.

I looked across at Danny. His eyes were really big, and he was holding on for dear life too.

Just when I thought we were going to get sucked into the wheels and die, the caboose went by with a whish. The clickety-clack of the wheels faded away. Everything got real quiet. I didn't move, but just laid there with my eyes closed, waiting for my heart to slow down.

Then a bird's wings whistled close by. The pigeon landed and cooed. Probably one of Mundo's. I heard crunching and the pigeon took off with another whistle of wings. I opened my eyes. Danny was standing over me. His clothes were black from the ballast shoulder. I pushed myself up, and we walked through our two grass trails back to our houses without saying a single other word.

I was thinking so hard about the dare that I didn't notice the police car until I nearly walked into it. I almost choked on my soda when I saw the Turk through the driver's side window. He had those sunglasses on again so I couldn't see his eyes. Then he took off the glasses, and I saw that they were blue like mine, but that probably didn't matter to him.

"*Orale*. Where are you *vatos* going?" *Pachuco* Spanish sounded wrong coming from a white man, especially a cop. The Turk was smiling a fake smile. His teeth looked like broken yellow crayons.

"We're just going home from Silverman's, Officer," Danny said. He sounded like a little kid.

"Officer, huh?" the Turk grunted. "Did you lift those sodas from Silverman's?" He pointed at the Nesbitt's in Danny's hand.

"No, sir. We bought them."

"Oh, you did, did you? And where did you get the money?"

This time it was me. "His uncle gave him two dimes, and my grandma gave me the rest."

The Turk pointed his sunglasses at me. "You sure you didn't take it off that tramp?"

My body felt a shock like touching a live wire.

"No, sir. My uncle." Danny said it, because I couldn't have said another word to save my life.

It felt like the Turk stared at us for an hour while we just stood there until his radio buzzed. Without taking his eyes off us, he said, "I'm going to check with Silverman's. If you're not telling the truth, I'm coming after you."

Then he pulled his sunglasses back on, put the car in gear and burned rubber taking off. At Sunset he took a left and headed away from us—and away from Silverman's.

When I got to my house, I went around to the side porch and into the kitchen. Something was different. Grandma had the radio on to a Mexican station. She was cooking at the stove and singing real happy along with the radio.

Then I saw a man sitting in a kitchen chair with his back to me. When the kitchen screen door slammed behind me, he turned around. He looked like my dad but smaller and skinnier and more worn out. And he had a bad haircut and tattoos on his neck and on the arm that he curled around the back of the chair.

Grandma turned to me about the same time. "Come and say hello to your uncle Rudy," she said. 'He just got home."

7

I wiped my hand on my pants and held it out for my uncle Rudy to shake.

"Manuel Maldonado, *a sus órdenes*," I said.

He smiled. His eyes were blue like mine, and he was missing a front tooth like my little sister Dorothy, but the rest of his teeth were real white. When he shook my hand, I saw a *pachuco* cross tattoo in that spot where his pointer finger and thumb met.

"*Qué hubo*, Little Man." His voice was higher than my dad's and sounded weak like he was sick or something. He said *liddo* like that tee-cat Marcel. Lino. Then I remembered I was supposed to tell Rudy that Lino came by looking for him, but something told me not to right then.

I stared at my dad-looking uncle until Grandma said, "Wash up and come and eat with us."

I looked at the stove. Grandma had made caldillo, Dad's favorite. When I got out of the bathroom, Rudy was already scooping up pieces of stew with part of a tortilla. Next to his plate was a cup of hobo coffee. Grandma saw me look at the cup. "He can't have alcohol. Parole board rules." When she said *parole board*, Rudy's shoulders slumped a little.

I sat down next to him. Grandma served me a small plate of stew. "I don't want you to spoil your appetite for supper, so just have one tortilla."

We ate without talking for a few minutes. Maybe Rudy was trying to think of something to say to me. The quiet didn't feel good.

"I'm going into seventh grade in September," I said.

"That's real nice." High, sick voice. "You any good in school?"

"I do okay. Not as good as Marco. That kid's really smart. He always gets way better report cards than me."

"Your dad was pretty good in school. You look a lot like him when he was your age." He kind of barked out his words like he was mad, but he couldn't already be mad at me. Maybe that's how people talk in prison. I didn't ask. I wanted to tell him that he looked like Dad too, but I didn't.

"Grandma says you're going to live with us," I told him. "You get to have my room. I'm going to sleep on the couch." By now Grandma had joined us at the table with her caldillo and coffee.

"Just until he finds his own place, right, *mijo*?" she said.

Rudy looked around the kitchen. "So. Has Sangra changed much?"

"I don't think so," Grandma said, "but you'll know better when you get out and about."

I liked the way that sounded. Out and about. I need to remember that. Out and about. Odds and ends. Rudy put one more piece of tortilla in his mouth. His dish was clean. He must have been hungry. He caught me looking at his plate.

"Home cooking. Nothing like it." He made that clicking sound with his mouth people do when they liked what they ate. When I looked at him, he winked at me. He shook a toothpick out of the little jar on the table and put it behind his ear, then he pushed his chair back and stood up.

"Now, if you'll excuse me, I'm going to get some shut eye." He said that like they do in the cowboy movies. I wondered if he got to see TV in prison. I wondered what prison was like, but I didn't ask. Rudy moved slow when he went over and kissed Grandma on the top of her head. I looked at her face. She was smiling but worry was standing right behind her smile.

Me and Grandma watched him walk to my old room. He looked shorter than Dad, but he was bent over so I couldn't be sure. And he walked kind of sideways, like those dogs you see walking down the street that got hit by a car but lived. You can't see any cuts or blood, but you know their insides are messed up, and they walk like Rudy.

"Prison has worn him down, so be nice to him," Grandma said and patted my hand.

I was watching cartoons when my mom and dad got home. Dad went to talk to Rudy right away. I thought he was going to hug and kiss him, but instead he told him to go out with him to the front porch. I could see them talking through the screen door.

Actually, I saw Dad talking. Rudy was sitting in the hobo chair and Dad was standing over him. I went to turn down the TV so I could listen, but Dad saw me. He opened the screen door and looked at me hard. Then he grabbed the big door and shut it.

I left the TV on, but I went to my old room. I looked out the front window. I could see Dad's face better from here, but all I could see of Rudy was the back of his head. He was staring down at the porch floor. He never looked up at Dad.

Dad walked back and forth and pointed his finger at Rudy or at the warehouses and mountains across the street. I could hear his voice through the window glass, but I couldn't tell what he was saying. It was the same voice he used when he told me Grandpa died. After a while, he stopped talking and started to walk to the door. I got up real fast and went back to the front room and pretended I was going into the kitchen so he wouldn't know where I'd been. He walked past me to his room without saying a word.

I went back to sitting on the couch facing the TV. In a minute Rudy came in. He winked at me again. Then he went into his room and shut the door soft-like.

Suppertime was weird. Grandma was quieter than usual. Her and Mom and Dad and Rudy ate in the kitchen. Me and Dorothy had to eat on TV trays in the front room, which was no fun because Mom didn't let us watch TV with supper.

"I think Daddy's mad at Uncle Rudy," Dorothy whispered.

"I don't think he's mad. He's just not happy Rudy's here."

"Why? If you were gone for a long time, I would be glad to see you."

I looked at Dorothy, and she gave me a quick little smile.

"Eat your supper," I told her. "I don't know what's going on, but Dad isn't mad."

I didn't want Dorothy to know that I was just as mixed up as she was.

8

Fourth of July was the best I ever had mainly because Dad let me set off fireworks. It was my first time lighting them and it made me feel big like Cruz. But it was good even before that.

In the morning the gang rode our bikes to Main Street in Alhambra to watch the parade. The parade itself was just pickup trucks with white girls waving flags in the back and a couple of high school bands that didn't sound very good and didn't march in straight lines.

When the Mission High band went by, I looked for Cruz who plays the saxophone and Danny's brother Rafa who plays trumpet. They also sing in the Casual Tones, the group Cruz started. There's four of them in the Tones. Cruz, Rafa, Big, and this *negro* who's named Brody who has a real low voice and sings the bass parts. Brody's the shortest guy in the group, but he has the biggest and deepest voice.

I know all their songs, all fifteen of them, because when they practice in Grandpa's garage, I go outside and watch them. Their songs all sound the same, mostly sad love songs. Rafa sings the main parts and Cruz plays the piano and sings backup.

Rafa marched by first. His face was red because it was a hot day and his uniform was heavy wool. He would take a breath just before he blew the trumpet and when he blew his cheeks would puff out like he had a tortilla stuffed in each one.

Then Cruz came past. The Mission High band wears green uniforms with a black satin sash that says Mission going across their chest with white fancy lines on their sleeves that look like the pin-striping on custom cars and those weird green hats with a big black feather on the top and white gloves and shoes.

Cruz hates those shoes. They're white like nurse shoes or baby shoes. On the third of July, I went over Cruz' house and watched him paint them with that white baby shoe polish and brush his uniform and shine his sax.

Cruz looked funny and he knew it. He tries to be so cool at school and around the neighborhood, but that day he didn't look very cool, and he knew all the girls from *Sangra* and Mission High would be at the parade and would see him trying to play his horn and march in step and walk in a straight line in those baby shoes.

The gang made fun of Rafa and Cruz. Little stood up and puffed out his cheeks playing a pretend trumpet. We made faces and acted like monkeys to try and get Cruz and Rafa to mess up.

In the afternoon Sangra had a block party on Main Street, the first time the neighborhood ever got together to celebrate the Fourth of July. It was Ted's idea. The men set up tables in the street under the big oak tree in front of Danny's house, and the ladies decorated them with red, white, and blue tablecloths. Mr. Marín, Elvira's dad from next door, cooked a goat in a hole the night before, and somebody else brought a roasted pig. Ladies brought beans and rice and salad and tortillas and cakes and pies and flán. Somebody in a pickup truck dropped off two kegs of beer, and somebody else brought two *tinas* filled with ice and bottles of Coke and gallons of Mother's Pride which is the cheapest soda you can buy.

About 6:30, everybody showed up to eat. Supper was supposed to start at 5 to leave time for the fireworks, but to Mexicans 5 is 6:30 so everybody was late at the same time. I skipped breakfast to go to the parade and didn't eat anything all day, so I was starving.

Before we could eat, three boy scouts—the Godinez brothers from Pearl Street—marched to a spot under the oak tree. The one in the middle, Andy, was carrying the American flag and they marched real sharp—not like the Mission High band. Men took off their hats and the ones in uniform saluted. Real loud, a man wearing an American Legion cap said, "I pledge allegiance to the flag..." and everybody joined him.

Then my Grandma shocked me. She started saying the "Our Father" in Spanish and Sangra joined in again.

After the prayer, people started laughing and talking. The same people who always do, ran to the front of the food line. I grabbed a Coke out of one of the washtubs and drank it while I waited in line with Danny.

We did some people-watching. Some of the men wore their old army uniforms even though they were too tight for them anymore. Ted didn't wear his. Some of the grandpas and grandmas wore their Sunday clothes. I saw Sonia in the middle of a group of guys. She looked fine. She was wearing a short skirt and a tight blouse and those tiny black shoes they call flats.

Rudy stood leaning against the oak tree. I watched different men go up to him and offer him a beer. He smiled and shook his head. Parole board rules.

By the time it was dark enough for fireworks, I was stuffed. I ate goat and chicken and beef and pork ribs and coleslaw and beans and rice and about eight tortillas and drank five Cokes. I thought my stomach was going to bust.

Me and Danny sat on my front porch wall and watched Sonia on their front porch. She was holding hands with some guy from the neighborhood I've seen before, except I didn't know his name or who his family was.

A rocket went off, and me and Danny watched it climb way up before it exploded and came down in a million little diamonds. The women clapped, and the men drank their beer.

"That's Rafa," Danny told me. "Him and my uncle Robert went down to T.J. and snuck back some Mexican *cuetes.*" He lifted his chin at the sky. "There's more where that came from."

The illegal firework show lasted about an hour. I got bored. Danny had to go home because the older guys were getting fresh with Sonia, and her dad didn't want her alone with them at home even though the block party was right in front of their house.

I lost track of Marco when he went to get another Coke from the *tina.* I knew Little wasn't there because his mom got into a fight with Big's mom, so the El Monte Street Gutis went home and the Sunset Avenue Gutis got to stay. They always fight at parties and funerals and weddings: one leaves and the other stays.

I went to where my mom and dad were sitting on a blanket in the front yard. Mom was holding Dorothy in her lap. My sister was asleep even though the firecrackers sounded like machine guns. I yawned and leaned against my dad's shoulder.

In a minute I must've knocked out.

When I woke up, I was on the couch under my blanket. I could feel the rubber sheet squeak under me. It was still hot because the front door was open. Through the screen door, I could hear far-away firecrackers go off once in a while. I guess the block party ended and everybody went home.

I looked at the open door of Rudy's room. He usually keeps it closed when he's inside. I felt thirsty so I got up and went to the kitchen for a glass of water. My teeth felt like there was a blanket on them from all the Cokes I drank at the block party. I was still in my clothes, and they had that stinky-nice firework smell.

I filled a glass with water from the sink and took a drink and looked at the clock on the stove through the bottom of the glass. It said 4 in the morning, still dark out the kitchen window. I put my glass in the sink and went back to the couch. I took off my clothes and covered myself and fell asleep again as soon as my head hit the pillow.

I woke up with a headache and wet sheets. The front room was filled with light, and I could feel my soaked underpants. I felt with my hand under the rubber sheet. The rough material of the couch was still dry.

I looked over at Rudy's door. It was still wide open. I got up and dug a clean pair of underwear out of my clothes box and went to the bathroom. The house was empty except for Dorothy who was working on a bowl of Frosted Flakes at the kitchen table.

"Where's everybody?" I asked her.

"Mom and Dad went to work, and Grandma's cleaning the sidewalk." A drip of milk leaked out the corner of her mouth and ran down her chin. "You smell like pee."

I moved away from her. "Where's Uncle Rudy?" She wiggled her shoulders and went back to her cereal.

I went into the bathroom to take a shower. Then I got dressed and pulled the wet things off the couch. While I was taking the stuff to the cuartito, Grandma came up the driveway holding an old broom and a dustpan.

"¿*Has visto a tu tío*?" she asked me. I shook my head. "He didn't come home last night." She put the broom and dustpan in the garage and took the peed things out of my hands. "I'll do this. You go eat breakfast."

Halfway through my Frosted Flakes, I heard meowing through the front screen door. I unlatched it and Danny followed me back to the kitchen.

"You want coffee?" I asked him. Grandma lets me drink coffee with milk and sugar when Mom's not home.

"No."

"What do you want to do?"

Danny just sat there.

"So, what do you want to do?" He moved his shoulders like Dorothy did when I asked her about Rudy. I finished my coffee and cereal and put the cup and bowls in the sink and wiped my mouth with a dishrag.

"Let's look for duds," I told him. Cruz told me him and Rafa used to find firecrackers that fizzled out, and they would put them all in a can and then throw a match in the can and they would explode. That sounded like fun.

↗

We only found one dud.

We were looking for more on the rightaway when we heard the horn of the 10:15 train. That's my favorite because it's really long and usually comes by slow on an east current. We backed off the rightaway all the way to the street because we were both still scared from when we did the dare. The 10:15 usually has cars from different train lines and the boxcars are different colors. Burlington Northern and Reading cars are green and Southern Pacific are kind of rusty red. Cotton Belts are bright red and Erie Westerns are blue.

I like the Great Northern cars best—bright orange with a white mountain goat painted on the side. Danny's favorite are the ugly brown Lackawannas. He likes the name, not the color.

The 10:15 was extra slow. It surprised us when the train stopped right in front of us. We got back on the rightaway and looked down the tracks to see why, but the tracks curve by Marco's house so we couldn't see to tell.

"Accident?" Danny asked.

The train goes above grade on a trestle over Rosemead Boulevard so an accident wouldn't happen there. It had to be down the tracks in El Monte because it was a strong current. There's been bad accidents where the tracks cross Del Mar Avenue. Cruz told me about one where the train hit a car on Del Mar and pushed it four blocks before the wreck stopped in front of Marco's house.

Cruz said it happened at night and Sangra was like an anthill when you pee on it, everybody running around all over the place trying to help the people inside the car. Police and ambulances came, but there was nothing they could do because the four teenagers inside were crushed to death. He said the wrecked car sat on the rightaway for three days until a tow truck finally hauled it away. Cruz said when him and Rafa went to see the wreck on the rightaway the day after, it reeked from booze.

Anyway, this train's caboose was about half a block up the tracks. We decided that if it was unlocked, we would look inside for flares. We walked to the back end of the train, but the bottom step of the caboose was over my head, so I boosted Danny up with my hands under his foot. When he was on the step, he pulled me up. We got on the porch and Danny tried the door. It opened so we went in.

I never been inside a caboose before. It smelled like oily smoke and stinky sweat. There were tools everywhere and a water jug hanging from a wall next to pictures of naked ladies and a smelly camping stove in one corner. I looked up at the part of the caboose that sticks out the top. I remembered Melinda Collison's train report said that was called a coopala.

Danny opened doors and lids and looked inside. I climbed up in the coop and looked down at my neighborhood and up the tracks at the Mission church through the dirty back windows and wondered what it would be like to be a crewman on a train.

"Bingo!" Danny said. Danny looked tiny from up where I was. He held up two flares in each hand. Suddenly a big jolt hit us. Danny fell on the floor, and the flares jumped out of his hands. I almost flew off the coop bench. The train started moving, and Danny looked up at me. His eyes were big like at the dare. With each breath I took, the train moved a little faster. I climbed down from the coop and ran to the open door and out to the porch where we got on. The Mission was getting farther and farther away. The ballast shoulder was far down and moving faster now and making me dizzy.

Before I knew it, we were passing Marco's house. I saw his mom in her back yard hanging sheets on the clothesline. And before I knew it again, I heard bells and saw a line of cars stopped behind the crossing arms on San Gabriel Boulevard. Me and Danny went inside and climbed back up to the coop bench.

"What are we going to do?" Danny yelled at me. His voice sounded like he wanted to cry. I wanted to cry too.

"What can we do?" I yelled back. Danny looked at me, then out the window. He turned his body and pulled up his knees so he could face front. I did the same, but faced back and the toes of our tennis shoes touched. We stayed that way for a long time.

9

All we could do was wait until the train stopped. Then we'd get off and try to find our way home. So we leaned back in the coop and stared out the windows. We could feel the train speed up across open spaces and slow down through towns on the east current. We watched farms pass us and factories and warehouses with broken windows and neighborhoods like ours. We went by trains stopped on side-outs waiting for us to go by, and we passed trains on the second tracks headed to where we were coming from and moving so fast they would've sucked us off the porch if we would've been out back.

We saw back yards with bed sheets and work clothes hanging on clotheslines. And yards filled with junked cars and trucks and chicken coops and barking dogs. Beautiful yards with vegetable gardens and yards that were pure dirt. Flower-filled yards and yards that had weeds growing to the top of the fence. Mothers carrying shopping bags with their kids behind them and tired-looking men holding jackets and lunch pails. Kids riding bikes on streets like Main Street that ran next to the tracks.

We saw a man in a *charro* hat training a horse in a ring and a naked man taking a bath in a big *tina* in his back yard. We passed cars stopped at crossings and drivers leaning on their arms and waiting for the train to pass and we heard the ding-ding-ding of the crossing bells get quiet when we left them behind.

And we saw boys. In every town we went through we saw boys lined up on the rightaway with rocks in their dirty hands to throw at us. We climbed down from the coop and went back out to the caboose's porch and watched boys throw their last rocks at our train until they saw me and Danny. We watched them just stand there staring at us and get smaller and smaller as we got farther and farther away. When they disappeared, we went back inside and climbed back up into the coop.

The caboose was hot and stuffy and we must've fell asleep. A rough hand shook my shoulder. I thought it was Cruz and right away I checked to see if I peed the bed.

No, I was wearing pants, and they were dry.

The hand shook me again. I opened my eyes. I wasn't in my bed or on the couch. I looked down to see a white man dressed in dirty work clothes with a red face and angry eyes and a curled lip.

"Get down from there!" he growled at me. I shook Danny and he woke up while I was climbing down. When we both got to the bottom, the man stood over us.

"What're yous doin' in the crummy?"

His crunched up face made me lose all my words.

"What're yous doin' in my caboose?" he growled louder. My mouth was stuck.

Danny talked for us. "We climbed up and the door wasn't locked. We went in and the train started moving."

The man jerked his head to the side. "Let's go."

He lifted us down from the caboose porch, dropped us on the ballast shoulder and shoved us to walk ahead of him. There were tracks going everywhere in the trainyard and they all had trains on them. There must've been a million cars in that yard. We zigzagged the tracks wherever there were breaks in the trains till we got to a mustard-colored building.

The trainman opened the door and pushed us in. Inside, another white man wearing clean overalls was sitting behind a desk reading a newspaper and smoking a pipe.

"Look what the cat drug in," the dirty trainman growled. I looked to see what the cat drug in. He was pointing at us. The clean man looked up from his paper. All I could do was stare at his hairy eyebrows and his eyes moving back and forth at us underneath them. The dirty man growled again. "Found 'ese two stowed away in my crummy."

The clean man's eyes went up to the dirty man. His eyebrows went up with his eyes as if everything made sense now. "Do you yard-rats have names?"

"Daniel Valdez, sir," Danny squeaked. I almost laughed because he really did sound like a rat, but I was too scared. The man turned his eyes to me without moving his head.

"Manuel Maldonado, sir." I didn't add *a sus órdenes* because he was white. My voice squeaked too. I could feel Danny's bony shoulder pressing against mine. I was glad my pants were dry.

"Where'd you yard-rats hop the train?" he asked us.

"San Gabriel, sir." He eyed me every time Danny said something, and every time I talked, he eyed Danny.

He waved his pipe in a circle at the ceiling. "You know where you're at?"

"No, sir." I didn't know too many train-towns after El Monte. I didn't know any really. His eyes shifted to the dirty man and his eyebrows dropped back down to their home.

"Colton," he said. "You're at Colton." I didn't know where that was, but the way he said it made me think it was way past El Monte.

The clean man leaned back in his chair. It squeaked. "Train-hoppin's against the law." He looked at the dirty man again. "It's a federal crime."

I looked at the floor. I was already going to prison for murder. Now I was going to prison for hopping the train. Dad was going to hate me like he hated Rudy.

The man opened the desk drawer and took out a pencil and a piece of paper and pointed over to a table. "Write down your names and telephone numbers. Your folks're going to have to come fetch you. If they won't, the Colton Police will." I remembered the paper the Turk made us fill out at Marco's house when we killed the hobo.

Danny took the pencil and paper. We walked over to the table, and Danny wrote while I looked around. The office was dark and dull. There was a blackboard on one wall covered in squares with numbers in them. Another wall had a bulletin board covered with papers. There was an old couch with a pillow and a folded blanket on one arm. The floor was wood and creaked when the dirty trainman walked around. And somewhere a clock ticked steady and loud like a kid tapping a pencil on his school desk during a test. From the way the light was coming in the windows, I figured it was around the time Grandma starts cleaning the supper beans.

Would she worry when she called me home and I didn't come?

"You hungry?" the clean man asked me, but I shook my head no. Danny was taking too long writing. The dirty workman opened the door and left. Danny slid the paper over to me, and I took the pencil. It was all wet with Danny's sweat. I wiped my hand and then printed my name and Grandma's phone number.

The clean man reached into a lunch pail on his desk and pulled out a sandwich wrapped in wax paper. He held it out and Danny took it right away. My stomach growled. I was sorry I said no. Danny unwrapped the sandwich and held out half to me. It was minced ham and cheese. My little sister Dorothy calls minced ham "mean Sam" because that's how it sounds when Grandma says it. She tells Grandma, "I want a mean Sam sandwich."

I wanted to laugh and cry all at the same time.

The door opened and the dirty trainman came back in. He put two Coke bottles on the table.

I looked at the clean man. "Go ahead," he said. I took one of the Cokes and Danny took the other. We sat on the couch with our sandwich and Cokes, and we ate slow and quiet.

The dirty man walked over and took the pencil and paper from the table and cleared his throat like he was going to spit, but he didn't. He looked at what we wrote and nodded his head to the clean trainman. Then the dirty man stepped out of the office and closed the door behind him.

I thought about how I usually never get to drink Cokes, but yesterday I had five and now another one today. Though this one didn't taste good. I couldn't really like it because all I could do was think about my dad and what was going to happen when he found out and had to come to wherever Colton was to get me after a whole day at work.

Before I knew it, someone was shaking my shoulder again. But this time it wasn't so rough. I opened my eyes and Dad was staring at me and blocking everything else in the room. He looked tired, and the blue of his eyes looked cold and hard as ice, like the night he told me Uncle Rudy would be coming home.

I looked around me. I wasn't in bed. I was sitting up, but I was on that couch covered in the blanket. It smelled like oil. Like the black gravel of the ballast shoulder on the rightaway. I checked, and my pants were dry. Danny was leaning against my shoulder snoring quiet.

"Let's go, Manuel." My dad didn't have that rumbly voice, didn't sound mad so much as tired. I shook Danny. He jumped.

"Your father's here," my dad told him. Danny looked around for his dad with big, scared eyes. "He's out in the truck," Dad said.

Dad thanked the clean man and said he was sorry for the trouble and took us out to Mr. Valdez' work truck. It was dark outside, and Mr. Valdez was just a dark shape sitting behind the wheel. When he saw us, he climbed out of the cab and started taking off his belt. I knew what was coming.

"You'll get yours when we're home. Get in the back," Dad said.

I climbed into the bed of the truck and sat there while Danny's dad gave him a belt whipping. I looked around at all the trains so Danny didn't have to see me watch him get it. I heard the belt hit its target and Danny yell "Oww!" each time. Five or six good ones.

He got into the back of the truck next to me when his father was finished. My dad handed me a blanket. I put it over us without looking at Danny. Two doors slammed and the truck motor started. We didn't talk all the way home.

Mostly, I thought about my dad. Worse than being scared of getting my belt whipping when we got home, I was ashamed of adding to his problems. Rudy didn't come home and Dad was probably going to have to go out looking for him once we got back to the house.

And if that wasn't bad enough, I was going to prison for murder and hopping the train. I wished I didn't have to be born so Dad would only have Dorothy to love and take care of and worry about. I brought him shame like Rudy, and I was sorry. But I couldn't go back in time and not get on the caboose. Or kill a hobo.

When we got back to San Gabriel, Mr. Valdez dropped us off. Dad got out of the cab. I climbed out of the bed.

"See you tomorrow," Danny said.

"*No vas a ver a nadien mañana*," Mr. Valdez said to him. Danny climbed out of the bed and got inside the cab. I watched the truck go two houses and turn into the Valdez driveway and go all the way into the back yard. Danny was looking back at me the whole way.

Dad wasn't more tired than mad. I got my own belt whipping in Grandpa's driveway behind the Chevy—a good one that burned my butt and three bad ones that hurt the most because I flinched and Dad's belt hit the backs of my legs. I left my butt alone but rubbed my legs to try and cool them off. I was expecting a hard chewing-out from Dad, but he pushed me into the house without saying a word. Mom and Grandma were waiting for us in the kitchen. I smelled caldillo and tortillas and coffee, but I just wanted to go to bed and make the stinging go away and forget everything that happened.

"*Regresó* Rudy," Grandma told my dad.

Dad still had his belt in his hand when he headed for the front room. I thought he was going to give Rudy a belt whipping too. He went into Rudy's room and slammed the door shut. He yelled at Rudy. I could tell by his voice that if Rudy was one of his kids he would have got belt whipped way worse than me and Danny.

I laid down on the couch and got under the covers and kept listening. I didn't hear Rudy's voice, but Dad roared a few more times, then it got real quiet. I turned on my pillow to face away just in time. Rudy's door opened, then slammed shut—then the same for Dad's door.

In a little while Mom came and took me to the bathroom. She had me pull down my pants and when she saw my legs, she clicked her tongue. She went to the kitchen and came back with the can of *manteca*. She scooped some of the lard with her fingers and spread it on the backs of my legs. At first it stung, but right away the burning started going away. She put soft pieces of flour sack on top of the lard and tied them with strips of the same material.

Then Grandma called me to her room and we knelt down and said the radio rosary. For Dad, Grandma said. By the time it was over, it was bedtime and my legs weren't burning as bad. Grandma took me back to the salón and tucked me in and blessed me over and over. Mom blessed me too and kissed me good night and her and Dorothy went into their room. Rudy's door was still closed. I waited for Dad to come out and bless me like he usually does.

I guess I fell asleep waiting.

10

If the government wanted to punish me for killing the hobo, all they had to do was keep doing what they were doing. It was past a month now since we killed the hobo and still the police didn't come get us. I didn't want to think we got away with it because I knew what would happen. I would get all relaxed and think we were okay, and then, just when I didn't think about the dead hobo and me and the gang in prison, that's when a bunch of police cars would pull up in front of our house and one of them—probably the chief of police—would yell through a bull horn, "Manuel Maldonado, your house is surrounded. Come out with your hands up."

And I would go out with my hands up and five or six cops would grab me and put handcuffs on me. They would take me out to the paddy wagon and stick me in the back. When I got in there Marco and Danny and Little would already be there, crying, all handcuffed behind their backs sitting on a bench. I would look around at all the women of Sangra staring at us from their front yards and shaking their heads at Grandma, and there would be a million kids on other kids' bikes who their moms sent to see what happened like they always do when there's a car crash on Del Mar or someone has a stroke like my Grandpa and the police or the ambulance have to come into the neighborhood. It wouldn't get into the *Herald Express,* but the whole neighborhood would talk about me and my family at the supper table and say what a rotten bunch we were and they always knew I was bad seed— look at Rudy.

That's what it would be like.

But it was near the middle of summer and still the cops didn't surround my house.

I saw the Turk about five times since the murder. Each time, he stared at me like he was the one making me wait to get arrested. At least I think he stared at me because I couldn't tell behind those sunglasses. I didn't really want to see his eyes anyway.

It was a long week being grounded. My legs didn't hurt any more from the belt whipping, but this was the fourth time this summer I was punished if you count getting kicked out of the San Gabriel Theater for throwing popcorn boxes at the screen and flying paper airplanes from the crying room in the balcony.

The crying room is upstairs near the restrooms and next to Mrs. Nevers' office who runs the show and who looks like the Wicked Witch of the West in "The Wizard of Oz." She usually keeps the crying room locked in the daytime, but once in a while she forgets to lock it.

Know-it-all Cruz told me that at night it's unlocked so

people can go up there to watch the movie if they can't get a babysitter. There's a window up there that they close when babies cry during the movie. That's why it's called the crying room. But Cruz tells me only couples who want to make out go up there at night.

Me and the gang go to the Saturday matinees because they show two movies and two cartoons after *Dangerous Playground*. Sometimes they have raffles between the movies. Danny's the only one in the gang who ever won. His prize was a squirt gun that looked like a tommy gun. He only used it once. His mom took it away after he shot *Doña* Tí with it and woke her up from her nap. She almost had a heart attack. He never saw it again.

Anyway, we got kicked out mainly because we're Mexican. It's the white kids that flatten out their popcorn boxes and throw them at the screen when the lights go out before the second movie starts, but they never get kicked out.

White kids never get kicked out, and Mexicans don't even buy popcorn. Mom gives me a quarter to get into the movie and have a snack, but I usually pay for Little's ticket because he's poor, and me and Danny buy Three Musketeers bars at Silverman's that we sneak into the theater. Candy bars cost five cents each in the lobby, but at Silverman's they're three for a dime. So I never have any money left for popcorn.

So. I got grounded for throwing the fruit at the hobos. That's one. Two was getting in trouble at the show.

Three was the smallest crime. I got room-grounded with no TV for one day for that. Me and Danny were sitting up in the club, and it was a hot and smoggy day. Those are the kind of summer days I hate, when you get kicked out of the house early, and the sun is hot and even the water from the outside faucet is hot and the smog is so thick and brown that if you didn't know the San Gabriel Mountains were there you wouldn't think there were any mountains at all.

But the club was cool and I stretched out on the cardboard in the green shade of the avocado tree. Danny was sitting cross-legged sorting through his baseball cards. He's always looking for cards of Mexican players. I tried collecting baseball cards, but I got bored so now I just chew the gum and save the cards for Danny except for two. One is the Bobby Avila card. He plays second base for the Cleveland Indians and he's Mexican. The other is the Raul Valdez Chicago White Sox rookie card. Raul signed the front for me. Danny has about a million Raul Valdezes.

Anyway, while we were up there, we heard the water start running in the bathroom underneath us. I didn't pay much attention at first, but then we heard humming and quiet splashing. We looked at each other. We both agreed: Yoci was taking a bath.

Danny put down his cards and crawled to the edge of the roof and hung his head over. I followed him. When I leaned over, I could see a little bit of the bathtub through the window. I wanted to see Yoci's *chichis* so I could to brag to Cruz, but all I could see was her feet. I watched them move in the soapy water. Her toenails were red. The splashes sounded happy and made me happy hearing them. She started singing a Mexican love song, but she didn't sing all the words. Sometimes she would skip words and just hum like she didn't really know the whole song.

Cruz' dad sings Mexican songs and plays his guitar at parties but mostly in bars. I guess that's where Cruz gets it from.

There was a loud splash, and I saw the feet go underwater. Then we heard the shower curtain rustle when Yoci got out of the tub. It was quiet for a minute. Then I saw the edge of a towel. I heard the drain plug pop and water start draining.

We crawled back to the cardboard, and Danny smiled at me. He held up his hands in front of his chest, and we laughed. I could hardy wait to brag to Cruz that I saw Yoci's *chichis* even if I didn't. That was on a Friday.

On Saturday morning Germán was on his front steps sharpening a machete with a file. I asked him what he was doing, and he told me Yoci told him she heard rats up on the roof. Big rats. They were probably eating *los aguacates*, he said, and he looked straight at me.

In the afternoon, my dad called me out to the front porch. He told me Germán complained about me and Danny bothering Yoci. I don't like to lie to my dad so I told him about watching her take a bath. Then he gave me a sex talk about men and women and babies. He looked like he didn't want to talk about those things, but he was forcing himself to do it.

I wanted to tell him Cruz already told me about that stuff using bad words I won't repeat, but I knew Dad thought he had to talk to me so I let him. I was room-grounded for the weekend, which was halfway over anyway.

The Monday morning after my room-grounding was the morning I spent with Rudy. I stopped calling him Uncle Rudy because he said it made him feel old. Then he laughed. I'm glad he said that because I don't call my aunts and uncles Uncle Ted or Tía Betty just Ted or Betty. And I never call Grandma *Abuelita* like my friends call theirs. She hates that, so I just call her Grandma.

Anyway, after breakfast me and Dorothy were watching cartoons when Rudy came out of his room wearing a suit. All I could do was stare at him. I never saw him look so nice. If I was a girl, I would've called him handsome. He looked like a movie star.

"Why you all dressed up?" Dorothy asked him.

Rudy pulled his lapels and smiled at her. "I'm going for a job interview."

"What's that?"

"That's when you talk to somebody and maybe they'll give you a job."

"Can I go with you?" I asked him.

"I don't think so," he said. "It's in Pasadena. And besides you know what your dad said."

Yeah. I wasn't supposed to hang around with Rudy.

"Can I walk with you to the bus stop?"

Rudy laughed. "I guess if we keep it hush-hush."

Dorothy looked at me with her face all scrunched up.

"He means this is our secret," I told her.

I don't think we got past Elvira's house when I asked Rudy about the war. Ever since I found out he was in the war, I wanted to know what happened to him and Ted.

"I don't talk about the war. It's over with and so am I."

We didn't talk again until we turned the corner.

"Why do you want to know?"

I blinked. "I killed a man and I wanted to know if you did too. In the war."

He stopped walking and looked down at me. "You killed a man?"

It took me about two seconds to decide not to tell him about the hobo after all. I smiled, and he thought I was joking and gave me a little punch in the arm, and we started walking again. When we got to the alley behind Silverman's, I started walking in but Rudy stopped me with his hand across my chest.

"Stay out of the alley."

"But I always go through here to get to Silverman's."

He shook his head. "Don't go through there no more. It's dangerous now."

I wanted to know what changed, but I thought I better keep my mouth shut.

When we got to the corner, Rudy said, "Tell you what. I need to think about how I want to tell you about the war. Give me a few days and ask me again."

We walked a little bit without talking anymore. Rudy whistled a Mexican song.

When we were almost at Silverman's, a car came up behind us. I heard the *pachuco* whistle. Both of us turned around. A big, dark-green Mercury pulled up to the curb just ahead of us and stopped. I counted five men in the car. The one riding shotgun leaned his head out the side window.

"*Q' hubo*, Rrruthee." It was Marcel. Lino.

Lino turned to me. "*Órale*, Liddo Man." One of the guys sitting in the backseat of the Merc stared out the side window at me with sleepy eyes almost shut, like he could barely keep them open.

Lino looked Rudy up and down. "Where you going all dressed out, *ese*?" He had a sleepy smile on his face but he didn't look happy.

"My business, *primo*. Not with the kid here. Watcha, I'll catch you later."

Lino looked up at Rudy, then at me, then at Rudy again. He mumbled something to the driver, and then gave Rudy that sleepy smile. "*Pués, hay te watcho, Nacho.*" He sleepy-smiled to me. "Later, Liddo Man."

The Merc pulled away but before it turned the corner in front of Silverman's, I saw a black face in the back window looking at us. It looked like Melinda Collison's brother Lawrence.

When the Merc disappeared, Rudy took me by my shoulders—not mad, but to make me pay attention.

"Look, Manny, those guys are bad news, so don't talk to them. Tecatos."

"How come they know you, Rudy?"

"Never mind that. Steer clear *y cuídate*."

"Yeah."

"And do me a big favor. Don't tell your dad about this, okay? He won't understand, and he'll get mad at both of us."

Yeah, hush-hush.

When the bus pulled up at the Del Mar bus stop, I watched Rudy get on and find a seat on my side. He held crossed fingers on both hands. I blessed myself to tell him I would pray for him. I watched the bus disappear up Del Mar Avenue, and then I headed home hoping I wouldn't see the Merc again.

I thought about Lawrence Collison in that car. Those other guys were a lot older than him. I wondered why he was with them.

$$11$$

Waiting for the police to come get us was like torture. So was carrying the sin around. I carried it with me wherever I went and whatever I did. Even after I took a shower, I could feel the dirtiness of that sin under my skin.

Thou shalt not kill was inside my heart like the ringing you get in your ears after you hear a loud noise close up—when it finally goes away you don't even know it because you got so used to it. Except this was in my heart, and I couldn't get used to it. I knew it wouldn't go away on its own, and I didn't want to die with that sin on my soul. I'm scared as hell of going to hell.

I wanted to go to confession, so I talked to the gang. We all agreed we'd go to the Mission on Saturday and confess together.

Confessions at the Mission are after 8 o'clock Mass. There's usually a bunch of sinners in line outside the confession boxes. This time there was a couple of men in their work clothes and the same old Mexican ladies who go to confession every Saturday and probably confess the same sins every week.

What sins can old ladies do?

And two little girls who looked like twins and who probably made their First Communion last May. And what sins could *they* do?

And a teenage boy and his girlfriend. You could tell they were boyfriend and girlfriend because they were holding hands and looking around like they were afraid somebody would recognize them. Little said they were probably going to confession because they made out in the crying room of the San Gabriel Theater.

The hardest part for me about going to confession is picking the right confession box. There's usually two priests hearing confessions on Saturday so there's two lines. And you don't ever want to get Father Simon Calderón. Father Simon's the pastor and everybody's scared of him.

At Sunday Mass, he tells the people from the altar that they aren't dressed good enough for church. He asks them why they wear their best for drinking and dancing on Saturday night but not for God on Sunday morning. And in his Holy Day sermons, he scolds the people, saying how come he only sees them in church on Easter and Christmas. And at communion, when half the crowd is heading for the doors, he tells them to get back in their pews and that Mass isn't over until he says so.

He's tough in confession too. Some priests let you slide when you just say you had an impure thought or you did something mean to somebody and leave it at that. But not Father Simon. If you just say you used bad words two times since your last confession, he asks you which words you used and when you said them and who you said them to. Or if you say you had three impure thoughts, he says what were those thoughts, and you have to spill the beans about every little thing like trying to see Yoci's *chichis.* He asks you who Yoci is and why did you want to see her *chichis,* and you don't know what to say. And he gives you hard penances like taking whatever you shoplifted back to Silverman's and saying a whole novena to *San Dimas,* the Good Thief.

So the trick is guessing which box Simon's in and then going to the other one.

I took a guess on the right-side line. Danny and Marco and Little followed me. I kneeled down and when the slider opened, I could see Father Simon on the other side of the screen with his wavy black hair and his prayer book open.

I guessed wrong.

But before I could get up and leave, he blessed me with his hand and said, "In the name of the Father and of the Son..." My heart was pounding, but I managed to squeak out, "Bless me, Father, for I have sinned."

The second hardest part is deciding which sins to open with. I'm never sure if I should get the big sins over with and finish with the small stuff like teasing Dorothy, or warm up with the little stuff and end with the real bad sins. The mortal ones.

This time I started small. I told him I missed Sunday Mass one time, and he asked me when and why. I told him Cruz misses Sunday Mass a lot, and I wanted to see what was the big deal so I faked being sick to find out. He didn't say anything, but he grunted like he didn't like my reason.

Then I told him about wanting to see Yoci's *chichis.* He asked me when this happened and where and how and why. I took a deep breath and told him about the club and my friend without saying Danny's name and Yoci taking a bath. I said about Germán and his machete, and it sounded like Simon was going to laugh, but he coughed instead.

Then I dropped the A-bomb on him. I told him I killed a hobo. When I told him that Father Simon stayed quiet a long time.

"Tell me that sin again," he said.

"I murdered a hobo."

Simon's head turned on the other side of the blurry screen. I'm glad it was dark on my side of the confessional, so he couldn't see my face and find out who I was.

"Tell me when and how you did that," he said. The light on his side of the confessional was behind his head and made him look like he had a halo like Jesus on holy cards. I told him about the hobo the same way I told my dad. When I was finished, I thought he was going to send me straight to hell.

"Did you know the man you say you murdered?" he asked me. It was weird how he said, "the man *you say* you murdered."

"No, Father," I said. "He was just a hobo on a train."

"He wasn't *just* a hobo on a train. He was a child of God!" Simon growled it like the dirty trainman. I was sure all the people waiting in line heard.

Then he cooled off, I guess, because he changed his voice. "Well, how do you know you killed him?"

I thought about it for only about a second. "I saw his dead body on the rightaway next to the tracks."

"Did you want to kill him?" That was a good question and the answer was easy.

"No, Father," I told him. "We were just playing."

He took a long time asking his next question.

"But how do you know you killed him?"

I got mixed up. I thought I already told him *I saw him on the rightaway.* Maybe Simon figured I was mixed up. He leaned close to the screen and changed the way he said the words.

"Why do you think *you* killed him? Could it be that maybe he just fell or was pushed off the train? It happens all the time."

I never ever even thought about *that*. As soon as we saw the hobo's dead body, we figured we killed him. What if we *didn't*? I could feel my heart trying to get out of my chest like one of Mundo's pigeons when you're holding it in your hands.

I was quiet a long time thinking about what Simon said. He grew up in San Gabriel too. He knew about the trains. And it was true that hobos fall off trains all the time. Cruz told me that a long time ago.

The confession box was getting hot, and it was getting harder to breathe, and I could smell the bad breath of all the people who ever went to confession inside that box. But none of that mattered. What mattered was that for the first time I was glad Simon asked so many questions.

I wanted to jump up and run out of the church to tell the gang.

Simon was looking back down at his prayer book. He smoothed the purple ribbon around his neck and said to the prayer book, "Did you tell your parents what you think you did?"

"Yes, Father."

"You didn't murder the hobo—the man on the train. If you didn't *want* to kill him, it wasn't murder. But you did throw fruit at the hobos. You did want to have fun at someone else's expense. Are you sorry for that?"

I was more happy than sorry, but I said, "Yes, Father."

"Then for your penance say one rosary for the repose of the man's soul."

I couldn't believe my ears. For all the stuff I did, all I got was a rosary to say!

If I was thinking straight, I would've knew I already did my penance with Grandma. Still, it didn't seem enough. But even if I didn't kill him, I'd say the rosary anyway. For him.

"Do I have to tell the police?"

Father Simon said, "I don't give legal advice. So if that's all, make a good act of contrition and get lost."

I said my act of contrition while Simon blessed away my sins. When I was finished Father Simon leaned against the screen and whispered, "Go in peace, Manny. Your sins are forgiven." I felt an electric shock go through me when he said my name. He knew it was me all along. And he still forgave me. I felt warm through my whole body, and I knew it wasn't because the confessional was hot. I thanked Father Simon and got up.

When I left the confession box, the cool dark of the adobe church felt good. I could feel my whole self shaking. I held the door open for Little and his eyes asked me how it went. I just smiled. I went out the side door to the church gardens to wait for my friends.

I sat on the edge of the fountain by the gift shop and thought about what just happened. I was still worried about the cops coming to get me, but right now I was all right with God, and I felt clean. I saw a dime on the ground. Somebody must've missed the fountain. I picked it up and threw it into the water. They probably did it for luck. I did it for them.

I didn't need luck.

As soon as we got to our bikes, I spilled the beans about my confession with Father Simon and the good news about the hobo. Little answered first.

"I'm glad you told him. I didn't have the guts."

Danny pulled his bike out of the rack. "Man's right, you know. Why didn't we think of it ourselves? Hobos fall off trains all the time. Everybody knows that."

Marco doesn't have a bike so he rides on my crossbar or Little's or Danny's wherever we go on bikes. He just stood there not getting on. "But how do we prove we didn't kill the hobo?"

Little tilted his head at Marco. "What do you mean?"

"What if the Turk says we were the ones who killed him?" Marco answered. "How do you prove you didn't do something?"

I didn't want to hear that. I wanted to go home happy that maybe I didn't kill a man, and the cops weren't coming for me. I didn't want to hear it after all the nights I laid awake thinking I was a murderer and all. I didn't want to think the Turk was still going to come after me.

Danny didn't help. "Marco's right. All the Turk wants to do is throw Metsicans in jail."

Marco must've seen the look on my face because he turned to Little.

"Can I ride with you?"

Little got on his bike and made room for Marco on his crossbar. We didn't say another word the rest of the way home.

This time the train horn sounded different. It sounded like Rudy's voice, and it was calling my name. A hobo who looked like Lino was sitting in the engineer's seat waving to me, and the engine headlight was shining on and off at our house. The shaking was real bad. Worse than I ever felt it before. The train engine was leaning and leaning and tipping over. And now it was sliding along the rightaway and across Main Street and sparks were flying all over the place and the whole time the engine horn was yelling "Manny, Manny, Manny!"

I wanted to jump out of bed and run, but my legs were paralyzed. My arms were getting squeezed and my right arm was twisted behind my back so I couldn't move it. I couldn't get up to get away from the train. Then the engine crashed into the front porch and sent chunks of cement flying and smashing the hobo chair. The roar was so loud I couldn't hear my own screaming. The train plowed through the screen door, then the wood door, then it exploded into the couch and smashed into me. It didn't hurt but I knew I was dying because I could feel my hot blood making a puddle under me.

"Manny! Manny!" The whole house was shaking now and I felt myself being lifted up. "Earthquake!"

I woke up in Rudy's arms. We were against the wall next to my clothes box. Rudy was crouching down and the whole house was shaking and rumbling. I saw the front wall of the house lean left and right in a way I didn't know walls could move. The little lamp hanging over the gas heater was swinging back and forth like the censer we use for benediction, only faster and in all different directions.

My dad came out of his room. His eyes looked like they were going to pop out of his head. He yelled at us "Don't move! Stay right there!" Then he ducked back into his room. I could hear Grandma screaming from her bedroom in the back of the house. I tried to get up to go look for her, but Rudy's arms held me tight.

"Stay put!" Rudy yelled at me.

I let my body go heavy in his arms. My underwear was wet and cold. I was shivering now and the pee burned the insides of my legs. Cruz would have cussed me out and called me Pee Baby and pushed me away, but Rudy held me tight. One of his hands covered the top of my head.

Earthquakes are weird. I been in about eight little ones that I remember—mostly at school. This earthquake seemed to last an hour. Half of me was scared and half of me was hypnotized by the shaking and rumbling. The house kept bucking like a bronco. It would have been fun if it wasn't an earthquake. I couldn't move. I was frozen still, wondering if it would stop or just keep getting bigger until it knocked our house down.

And besides, Rudy was holding me tight.

The hard shaking finally stopped, and Rudy let me loose. I stood up to go look for Grandma, but then another quake started, and I jumped back in Rudy's lap. The house started shaking again just as bad as the first time. I heard dishes fly out of the trastero and smash on the kitchen floor.

The second quake finally got smaller and smaller and the rumbling got quieter and quieter like a train disappearing down the tracks until everything was still again. We waited, me and Rudy. Then Mom came out of her bedroom dressed in a bathrobe and slippers. Dad came out behind her holding a blanket bundle I knew was Dorothy. He jerked his head toward the front door.

Rudy told me "Let's go outside," and wrapped me in a blanket and lifted me up. I didn't want to be carried at first, but I didn't want to go outside in wet underwear trying to hold a blanket around me either.

We stood in the middle of Main Street. I was really surprised there was no train crashed on the tracks or on the rightaway or on the houses or in the street.

Dad went back in the house and came out carrying Grandma's rocking chair with Grandma wrapped in a blanket walking behind him. Her fingers were moving the beads of her rosary outside the blanket. When Dad set the chair down next to me, she sat in it and touched the top of my head to tell me she was all right.

The streetlights were out and the houses were dark all up and down Main. I could hear the sirens of fire engines north of the tracks. More families came out of their houses and joined us in the street. The quakes scattered a million oak leaves on the ground in front of Danny's house.

I didn't want anybody to see me in my peed underwear so I kept to myself.

Danny came over to me. If it was anybody else I would've told them to scram, but Danny already knew I peed my bed, and I couldn't help it, and he never made fun of me.

"Man, that was a big one." He smiled at me. I wasn't sure if it was a real smile or if it was one of those fake ones when you need to cry but don't want to. It didn't matter to me with Danny. "You guys okay?"

"I think so. I pissed my bed. I thought the train derailed and chopped my legs off. I thought the piss was my blood!" We both laughed to hear me talk like Cruz.

Danny said, "Sonia ran out of her room naked, then she ran back in to get dressed. That was funny as hey-yell."

I tried to imagine what Sonia looked like naked. When I found her sitting next to her mom on the curb, she was wrapped in a blanket from head to toe. I couldn't tell if she was wearing clothes underneath.

My dad and other Main Street men were standing together away from the women and kids. Nobody was laughing. The whole scene was so different from Fourth of July when everybody was having fun.

Another earthquake hit, but it was a little one. Still, I heard women scream. A couple of babies cried. Dogs barked and the wires swung like jump ropes between the telephone poles on the rightaway. After a while the men left their group, and all the families went back to their houses. I shook hands with Danny and told him I'd see him tomorrow.

"Today is tomorrow!" he told me. He showed me the watch he got from his *ninos* on his last birthday that glows in the dark. The glow said 4 am.

I went back to my bed on the couch after my shower. The

sheets were already changed. I climbed under the blanket. In no time I was dreaming again. This time I was on a boat on the ocean and the waves rocked me up and down real gentle.

I woke up when I smelled coffee. I checked myself and even though I was dry, I had to pee bad. I put on my pants and went to the bathroom. I came back out to the kitchen expecting to see broken dishes all over the floor, but it was clean.

Mom and Dad and Dorothy were sitting at the table eating breakfast.

"Why aren't you at work?"

"Work told us not to go in." Mom works in a sewing factory downtown. She's really good at sewing and makes all of her and Dorothy's clothes and some shirts for me. One time I saw a cowboy on TV and I asked Mom if she could make me a shirt like his. She did, and it was perfect. She told me once that she loved to wear nice clothes as a girl, but they were too poor so she learned how to sew, and she made her own clothes. She can look at any dress or shirt or anything and make a copy of it on her Singer.

Betty tells me Mom could've been a fashion designer in Hollywood, but Mom laughs when she hears that. Once I asked her why she didn't stay home like Danny's mom or Marco's mom or Betty. She told me she got a job making parachutes at a factory in Long Beach during the war and found out she liked working outside the house. And besides, her and Dad were working and saving to build a house on the empty lot Grandpa gave them behind Grandma's.

Dad drops Mom off downtown then goes to work in Lincoln Heights at a plant that makes kitchen cabinet knobs. Dad got the job in the plant after he came home from the war. He told me they made him a cook in the war, and he got sent to guard Alaska from the Japanese. I asked him if he killed any Japs, and he said he didn't think so unless they sneaked into his camp and ate his food.

Anyway, I guess I was sleepy from last night because I sat down across from Dorothy and just stared away at nothing.

"We have no more bowls, so you have to eat *huevos revueltos*." Grandma was standing at the stove pointing a wooden spoon at me. Scrambled eggs were fine, especially when they were wrapped in a warm tortilla. "You want coffee?" I nodded my head. Mom made a face at her.

"Where's Rudy?" I asked my dad.

"Out. And this time I'm not going to go looking for him," he barked. Then he looked at me and his voice was softer. "School start next week?" Mom already measured me for new school shirts, but we still had to buy corduroy pants. I didn't want to think about school until I had to.

"Is the house okay?" I asked Dad.

"As far as I can tell, the only thing wrong is the power's out. But I'm going to spend today looking everything over to make sure."

Grandma set a cup of coffee in front of me.

Mom asked me, "Are you ready for seventh grade?"

"Yeah, I guess."

"You don't sound ready. You know eighth grade comes next, then high school. Have you thought about that?" I looked at Mom but didn't answer her. A plate landed on the table in front of me with two rolled tortillas. I could see scrambled eggs peeking out the open tops. I took a bite of one so I wouldn't have to answer.

The truth is I do think about high school a lot, and I don't like the idea. I see high school guys like Cruz, and they never look happy. They go around trying to look so tough and cool. They look like they never have fun. I watch them when they dance at lunchtime out in the high school patio which is next to our play yard. Even when they dance with the girls, the boys all look like they're doing something they don't want to.

Cruz is the worst one. He acts like nothing's ever right. I used to tell him things I thought were funny or interesting, but he always said it was stupid or I was stupid so I stopped telling him anything. I keep those things to myself until I can tell the gang. They're my age, and we still have fun and act goofy and don't care.

But the high school guys never do. That's why I don't want to go to high school.

I was just starting on my second egg taco when Betty came into the kitchen.

"Those were some shakers, weren't they?" She sounded

happy. Betty always sounds happy. She could say, "That was quite a bad accident," and sound happy. She went to the stove and gave Grandma a kiss and poured herself a cup of coffee. She leaned against the sink and took a sip.

"Those wine glasses Ted brought back from Europe are all gone now. Broken into a million pieces." I knew the glasses she was talking about. She took them out of her trastero and showed them to me one time. There were six glasses on a glass tray and each one was a different color. She showed me how when she put a drop of water on the rim and moved her pointer finger around the edge, the glass made a ringing sound. "That's how you know it's real crystal," she told me.

"All six of them?" I mumbled.

"What?"

I swallowed the wad of egg and tortilla in my mouth. "All six of them?"

"Yeah. I guess Ted's just going to have to take me to Europe to get some new ones."

She laughed. She said she wished that was all Ted had brought back from the war. I didn't know what she meant, but I let it slide. Grandma turned from the stove.

"Is Ted coming over? There's plenty of food."

"No, he had to go to the market. People need to eat, he says. And the power's out all over. They're probably going to have to give away all the meat and dairy before it spoils. Did you lose anything?"

Grandma pointed her wooden spoon at the trastero. "Some bowls and a cup. Nothing important. My good things are down there in boxes." I knew about the good plates and cups. I found them one day when I was snooping around. I never saw her use them, not even for Grandpa's funeral. I don't know what she's waiting for.

"Say, Manuel. I want to ask you. If the show is still on, is it okay if I take Manny with me?" She was talking to my dad. She called him Manuel English-style.

I heard a rumble and felt the kitchen move up and down slow and gentle like a fresh sheet spread on a bed. Betty fell back against the sink and grabbed the edge of the counter. "Oh, Jesus!" she yelled. Dad grabbed Dorothy's hand. Mom grabbed mine and Grandma held on to the stove. By the time I looked at everybody, the quake was over. It was an aftershock.

"I hate these aftershocks," Mom said. "I'm always afraid they're going to be big like the first one. I don't know how they tell if it's an after-quake or a new one. Won't they cancel the show because of the quakes?" she asked Betty.

"They probably will. But it's still two weeks away. If they don't, I'd like to take Manny with me. Ted doesn't want to go. He said he's too old for teenage dances, but I promised Cruz I would. To show him support."

Cruz and the Casual Tones were going to be part of a big rock and roll show. He said the Tones went to Los Angeles and sang for some man who signed them up for the show.

It was going to be at the Legion, and they were going to get ten dollars for singing three songs. Ten dollars! Cruz would tell people they were going to sing with a famous *negro* group called Don and Dewey. I heard Don and Dewey's records on the radio station that plays *negro* music. All the teenagers in Sangra listen to the *negro* station. If you walk down Main Street, all you hear is *negro* music or Mexican music. Cruz says the *negro* station plays better music than the white stations.

Everybody Cruz told about the show wished him good luck. He didn't tell them there was seven other groups singing that night before Don and Dewey. I guess that wasn't important.

Anyway, Dad looked at Mom and then at Betty. Dad growled at Betty, "We'll see. He's been getting into a lot of trouble lately. I don't know if I can trust him."

I really wanted to go—not to hear the Tones. I hear them practice in Grandpa's garage all the time. I wanted to be with Betty because she's the only grown-up I know who's fun. She taught me how to dance the boogie-woogie and bee-bop when we all went to somebody from Sangra's wedding reception at the Arbor Hall.

At first when my dad said, "We'll see," I thought I had a chance. But when he talked about trouble, I thought about the hobo and Colton and Yoci, and I didn't blame him for not trusting me. I looked at him, and I tried to imagine what his face would look like if I was looking at him through prison bars.

Or maybe he would never visit me like he never visited Rudy.

"Did you see Rudy on your way over here?" Dad asked Betty.

Betty rinsed her dirty cup and put it in the sink. "No, why? Is he AWOL?"

"He was supposed to go into L.A. with me today about a job I found for him."

"I don't imagine anybody is open for work today with the earthquake and everything," Mom said. "Besides, you could use the day off. You didn't sleep all night."

Dad growled again at Betty, "Well, when you see him hanging around Silverman's, tell him I'm looking for him."

Betty rolled her eyes. "Whatever's eating you, keep me out of it! I'm going home." She walked across the kitchen and out the screen door without saying goodbye to anybody.

I put what was left of the egg taco in my pants pocket for later and ran out after her. "Why is Dad mad at everybody?" I asked her.

"He's just mad at Rudy."

"Why? What did he do?"

Betty stopped walking. She looked around, then took my hand. We sat down on Grandma's little bench under the fig tree.

"Honey, Rudy didn't...Rudy's sick."

"Is he a *tecato*?"

Betty looked kind of surprised. "How do you know?"

I thought about what I had promised Rudy. Hush-hush. But that was to Dad, not Betty. "He sort of looks like them in a way, and a week before he came home a *tecato* named..." I tried to remember his name. I tried remembering what he looked like in front of Grandma's house and in the Merc in front of Silverman's. "...Lino. This *tecato* named Lino came to our house asking for him before he came home from Folsom."

Betty patted my hand. "Honey, don't call them that name. It sounds bad. They're sick. Some of them die because of that heroin drug. Somebody gives them marijuana to try, and they like how it makes them feel. Then those people give them heroin, and they get hooked on it, and they can't get away from it." I got what she was talking about. I thought about Cruz smoking marijuana.

Betty squeezed my hand, and I came back to her. "I'm going to tell you something but I need you to promise me you'll never— ever—tell another person, okay?" Another secret and another promise. I didn't want to make another promise to a grown-up, but it seemed like Betty needed to tell me worse than I wanted to know.

She squeezed my hand harder, and it almost hurt. "When Ted came back from the war, he was pretty messed up. He told me he saw and did some horrible things. Some of his buddies didn't make it home. And he was hurt pretty bad."

Right away I remembered his scar. One time last summer we all went to Marrano Beach to go swimming and have a picnic. Marrano Beach isn't really a beach. That's just what Sangra calls this place along the Rio Hondo where mostly Mexicans go. Marrano Beach is a bend in a stream that flows into the San Gabriel River.

Ted was in his trunks. A red scar ran across his chest and left arm from the top of his shoulder to his elbow. It wasn't as dark as my port-wine stain, but it was really red and almost looked like a port-wine stain except it was kind of crinkly and had white streaks.

Anyway, Betty said, "When he got home from the war, he was real quiet and angry all the time. He didn't want to do anything but sleep. Sometimes he would have real bad nightmares, and he would wake up screaming and crying. I know this sounds scary, but I want you to know something important.

"Eventually, Ted was able to go outside our house and even across the street to Silverman's. He met some guy there and pretty soon Ted was coming home late smelling like marijuana. And after that he wasn't so mad, and his nightmares weren't so bad, but I was scared he was becoming a drug addict. I don't know what happened, but the guy he was hanging around with got arrested and put in jail, and Ted stopped smoking reefer. He still has bad dreams and sometimes he drinks too much but at least he's not an addict.

"I'm telling you all this about Ted because I think Rudy saw and did some bad things in the war too. Even if he didn't get a Purple Heart like Ted, you know?

"Your dad's very angry at Rudy and I understand that, but you and I don't have to be. We have to love him and pray for him to get well." I wanted to tell Betty that I already do love him and I already do pray for him, but I didn't want to butt in when she was talking.

Betty patted my hand. "I should've asked you if you wanted to go to Cruz' show with me before I asked your father. That was disrespectful. I'll ask you now. Would you please go with me?"

I think that's one of the reasons I love Betty so much. She treats me like a kid but she doesn't make me feel bad that I'm a kid. She's not like all the other grown ups. She never makes me feel like I'm in her way or do things that bug her. She makes me feel like I'm her friend.

"Sure, Betty. If you want me to go with you, I will. But won't you feel stupid going to a rock and roll show with a kid?"

She smiled at me and stood up.

"If they let a *vieja* like me in, who cares how old my date is?" She laughed. "But do me a favor. Stay out of trouble until the show, okay?" She laughed again and mussed up my hair. I watched her walk out the back gate and disappear. Then I took the taco out of my pocket and finished eating it in the shade of the fig tree.

14

Two days after Betty invited me to Cruz' show, Danny invited me to go with him to see the Man From Mars. He read in the newspaper that the Man would be on display at the San Gabriel police station for one week only. I don't have to tell you I wasn't crazy about the idea.

Once Cruz told me about the Man From Mars. That he robbed some markets in San Gabriel. That he was called the Man From Mars because he would go in the stores dressed in black clothes and a black football helmet and a gas mask and cartridge belts across his chest like the Mexican bad guys in the movies. He would point his shotgun at the store people and make them give him money. Then he would run out and escape down a manhole and get away through the storm pipes. He robbed five markets before a cop killed him in a shoot-out at the Boy's Market on Valley Boulevard.

Guess who killed him? Yeah. He got some award from the city for bravery or something.

Anyway, they don't put the real Man From Mars on display. He's dead and buried somewhere, so they use this dummy wearing the helmet and the other stuff but not the shotgun. This would be our first chance ever to see him.

But what if the Turk saw us there? I remembered laying up in the club and thinking that the cops were going to come get us. Now Danny wanted us to walk into that police station right under their noses.

At first we thought the station was closed. We tried the glass door, but it wouldn't open. Then a man in a suit walked out and before the door could close we slipped inside. There was a desk in the middle of the hall, but nobody was there. Danny pointed down the hall and there at the end was the Man From Mars standing straight wearing his bandit clothes like those dummies in the JC Penney window. There was one light shining on him and that made him look even scarier. Still, we walked up real close, real slow.

Close up, the Man's clothes were nothing special, just work clothes—like Dad's, except black. The dummy had on black gloves and black motorcycle boots that laced almost to its knees. The gas mask he was wearing was kind of like the one Cruz bought at an Army-Navy store for last Halloween. The clothes were too big for the dummy and hung loose and made it seem more funny than scary. It's weird how some things look scarier far away than close up.

It was like that with the hobo too. When we first saw him on the rightaway, he was real scary, and we didn't want to get closer. But when we did, it wasn't so bad if you don't count that he was dead. He just looked like a man sleeping on the ground except for his broken arm all twisted behind him.

"Look there." Danny pointed up at the football helmet. It

was made out of leather and there was a spot in front that was darker than the rest with a hole in the middle. "That's where the Turk got him."

I don't know how far away the Turk was when he shot the Man From Mars, but he hit the bull's eye. There was a picture of the Turk on the wall next to the dummy. He looked a lot younger than in real life. In the picture he was standing over the Man From Mars and pointing at a shotgun on the floor next to the Man. That's how he looked on the rightaway standing over the hobo except older.

"What are you two doing in here?" The hallway made the voice echo. We jumped. We turned around and saw a policeman standing behind the desk.

"Nothing, sir," Danny answered in that little-kid voice of his. "We just wanted to see the bad guy." The police officer grunted and sat down at the desk. "Well, don't touch anything." We took one last look at the Man From Mars. I thought about how he just stole some money and the cops shot him dead, but we maybe killed a man, and we were going to walk out of the police station like free men. That made me feel sick to my stomach. I threw up on the grass in the park across the street. I barfed again and again until my stomach hurt even though nothing came up. Danny put his hand on my back and rubbed it, but it didn't help.

"What's the matter?"

I tasted that awful sour taste of barf. "Going in there must've gave me *asco*."

Danny sat down on a bench and waited for me to feel better. When I did, I went over and sat next to him. "Maybe we shouldn't've went in."

"He's dead and there's nothing we can do about it," Danny said. I didn't know if he was talking about the Man From Mars or the hobo.

I only saw Rudy one time during those two weeks. It was early in the morning. I know because the pee woke me. I was pulling the wet sheets off the couch when somebody came into the front room dressed all in black. I guess I was sleepy because all I could think of was that the Man From Mars was in our house. My heart started pounding in my chest and I almost peed again. Then the man in black went into Rudy's room and closed the door.

The second thing that happened during those two weeks was we started school. Besides not wanting summer vacation to end, what I don't like about September is wearing new corduroy pants. At Mission Grammar we wear uniforms and the boys have to wear those salt-and-pepper corduroys. The weather's always hot in September and those new pants give me a rash between my legs that burns like hell when I pee the bed. Plus they make that stupid zip-zip sound when I walk.

My mom made me three new school shirts. I asked Grandma if she could starch and iron my new shirts so they would be crispy for school, and she did.

I waited on the front porch for Danny and Marco to pick me up. Danny was in my grade, and Marco was a year behind and starting sixth grade. Me and Danny and Marco talked about all the stuff that happened during the summer. The heat wave made it feel like it was still summer, but the sunlight didn't look the same as in July and the first part of August. It was still real smoggy, so I couldn't see the heart on the mountain. And some of what happened in the summer was getting smoggy too. We had to talk about the hobo, but none of us wanted to say much about him, so we sort of agreed without words to skip the subject.

Danny asked Marco, "Who you getting this year?"

Marco's answer was short. "Mary Thomas." Sister Mary Thomas isn't as cool as Sister Francis Assisi, but still she loves art.

I told Marco, "You're going to get to do a lot of art projects."

We walked a little bit more. Then Danny said, "This is the year we get Capone."

Her real name is Sister Alphonsus, but the high school guys call her Capone. I guess because she's Italian, and they say she can kill you with just a stare. Capone is the toughest teacher in our school. If we could just get past her for seventh, eighth grade would be a breeze. At least that's what Cruz and Rafa told us.

Keep this hush-hush, but I love Sister Francis Assisi. I wish she could've been our teacher this year too. And she's beautiful. She has blue eyes and white skin and red lips and rosy cheeks like the 'Maculate Conception statue in Grandma's saints case.

And can she throw a football! Last year during lunchtime some high school guys were passing a football around on their side of the fence to show off for the girls. The ball flew over to our side and Francis Assisi asked one of us to bring the ball to her. She took it and told a high school guy to go long. She threw a perfect spiral that went so far he had to run hard to catch it.

Sister Francis Assisi taught us that God loves us and wants us to love him. She said our prayers are like love letters to God. She says God is a mystery, that we are all children of God, and we should love each other like brothers and sisters.

I think about the Turk and how I wouldn't want a brother as

mean as him. Cruz is mean to me, but he's just my cousin, and he's nothing compared to the Turk. Sometimes I worry that I'm going to go to hell for something bad I did even though Francis Assisi tells me God forgives every sin if we're sorry we did it. I always ask God to forgive me when I pray the radio rosary with Grandma. And I know God forgives me when I go to confession. Even to Father Simon.

We met Little at the schoolyard gate and walked with him over to where the seventh graders line up. Little's dad went back to Mexico after the Fourth of July and Little told us he still wasn't back. He said his mom said Mister Guti probably got stopped by the border patrol as a wetback.

Big's mom said he probably had to check up on all his other families down there, and it would probably take some time. We all laughed.

I told Little about seeing the Man From Mars with Danny, and he got kind of mad we didn't invite him. But he got over it pretty quick and before long we were laughing about his dad again and marching to our classrooms to a record on the loudspeaker of some song that Cruz plays with the Mission High School marching band.

15

Capone was as hard as they said. I already had too much homework. My book bag felt like a ton of bricks. But I stayed out of trouble.

On the Saturday afternoon of Cruz' show, I took a shower and splashed on some of Dad's Old Spice. I put on a crispy, new sport shirt Mom made that Grandma starched and ironed for me, and I combed my hair until my arm hurt. I looked pretty good in the mirror, so all I had to do was wait for Betty.

When Betty pulled up in Ted's car and honked, I ran out to the cuartito to say bye to Mom. She blessed the sign of the Cross on my forehead and told me to be good. I looked for Dad to get a blessing, but Mom said he went looking for Rudy. On my way to the front, Grandma stopped her watering and blessed my forehead in Spanish. Before I knew it, I was sitting next to Betty in the front seat. And before we knew it, we were at the Legion.

That's what they call the El Monte American Legion Stadium. But it doesn't look anything like a stadium. More like the Mission High School auditorium, just way bigger.

When we got out of the car Betty put her hand through my arm. Any place else and with anybody else, I would've wiggled away like a worm, but because it was Betty, I let her. I could smell her perfume even though there was cigarette smoke everywhere from the teenagers hanging around in the parking lot.

I saw teenage couples holding hands and kissing each other like there's no tomorrow and lots of custom cars—real nice paint jobs and some lowered so much they almost scraped the ground. One time Cruz told me those kinds of pipes that run along the sides of the car are called "lakes pipes," but when I asked him why, he told me to shut up and stop asking stupid questions.

On some cars the wheels had spinners, hubcaps that twinkle like stars when the wheels turn. Cruz thinks they look tough. When he gets a car, he says he's going to put on lakes pipes and spinners. There were a few jalopies too, but I don't like those too much. Neither does Betty. Jalopies don't have fenders and some don't even have tops.

Betty pointed to one without a top and said, "Why would a girl go through all the trouble of fixing her hair if she was going to have to ride in one of those?"

We waited in the ticket line a long time, but we finally got to the window. The whole time the lady in the window kept staring at my port-wine stain. I could feel her eyes on me like I do every time people stare at me. Her stare started at my collar and went up my neck and across my face and into my red hair like a crawling bug.

The inside of the Legion smelled like old cigarettes and B.O. You'd think they'd open the windows during the daytime to let out the B.O., but in a little while when the show started and the teenagers were dancing, I forgot about the smells.

The place got packed real fast. Me and Betty went up and sat in the balcony straight across from the stage. At first there was plenty of room to spread out, but when the balcony got more crowded we had to move closer together, so pretty soon we were sitting so close I could feel Betty's hip press against mine which felt good.

After most of the people were inside, they closed the lights. The place went black and the teenagers started yelling and hooting like they do at the San Gabriel Theater before the movie starts, and the white kids throw stuff at the screen, and the Mexicans get kicked out. In a minute a spotlight went up on a white man wearing a white tuxedo standing on the stage holding a microphone.

"Are you ready to rock and roll?" He yelled it so loud into the mike that I had to cover my ears with my hands. The teenagers yelled and screamed back at him. They sounded like at the Smith Park pool when people are yelling, but you're underwater.

"I can't hear you. I SAID, 'ARE YOU READY TO ROCK AND ROLL?'" The teenagers yelled even louder than the first time. The curtains opened and a band started playing. Spotlights shined different colored lights on the people on the dance floor. I almost got dizzy from looking down at them dancing and moving around like ants when you pour gasoline on their ant hole.

The band was four *negros*. They played three jive songs without singing. After them the man with the microphone announced a singing group that sang one song. They looked real young and real nervous, and they weren't very good. They kept looking at each other like they didn't know what to do. After their song, people clapped but some people booed. One of the singers looked like he was going to cry, then they left the stage.

The Tones were the fourth group to take the stage. The man with the microphone said, "Let's give an El Monte Legion Stadium welcome to San Gabriel's very own, 'The Casual Tones.'" He said that for every group, like "Baldwin Park's very own" or "Azusa's very own." When Betty saw the Tones come on stage, she poked me in the ribs with her elbow. Her hip wiggled.

They looked like I never saw them before. They were all wearing the same thing: starched and ironed khaki pants and French toe shoes and the shirts my mom made them. I remember going to downtown L.A. with Cruz and Mom to pick out the right material for the shirts. It took us a whole Saturday going into all the fabric shops on Maple Street until they found the perfect material. It was deep blue with silver threads going through it.

Mom told Cruz that the fabric would look great when the spotlights shined on it. The neatest part was that she sewed "CT" in fancy letters with her Singer on the shirt pockets. No other group had that. Cruz used his birthday money to buy Florsheim French toe shoes, except they weren't real Florsheims, and they squeaked when he first walked in them. They were cheap look-alikes, but Cruz didn't care. He told me nobody would know when he was on stage. He brought them over to show Grandma. He spit-shined them on her side porch till I could see my face in the toes, and then he put them to bed in their box.

The Tones sang a slow love song, then a fast one, then another slow love song that Cruz wrote himself. After the first song they didn't look nervous anymore. Then Rafa—who sings the high parts—made a joke and the crowd laughed. When their set—Cruz, who knows everything, told me that's what it's called—when their set ended they got a good clap from the crowd.

I asked Betty if we were leaving now that we saw the Tones,

but she said no. She wanted to see a couple more groups, but we wouldn't stay for Don and Dewey. Then she told me she left her sweater in the car and asked if I thought I could go by myself to get it for her. I asked her why she wanted a sweater. The big crowd of teenagers and the fact that there weren't any open windows made me sweaty just sitting there. She said that the air outside would be cold when we left, and she didn't want to catch a chill. She handed me her car keys and told me to be careful and come right back.

Betty was right. When I went outside, it was foggy and cold. About halfway to the car I had to pee, so I looked around for a dark place where I could do my business. I found a shed nearby. I went behind it and unzipped my pants as fast as I could and let the pee shoot against the wall. There was a light shining somewhere because I could see my pee bend like a rainbow and make a dark puddle that steamed in the light and fog. When I was done, I zipped back up.

But before I could turn around, I heard a voice behind me. I pushed myself into the wall of the shed and hoped whoever it was didn't hear me. The voice was rough and hard, full of anger. The voice that answered was weak and scared. Then there was another voice that sounded real familiar. They were arguing and using lots of dirty words. They were men's voices, not teenagers, and I recognized two of them. One was Rudy's. He must have been tired or drunk because he was talking real slow. I couldn't understand most of what he was saying.

The other voice—the hard one—was Lino's. He wanted money. *Now.* The voice I didn't recognize said he would pay him.

"When?"

"A couple of days."

Then I heard shoes scraping on the ground and kicks and punches landing that sounded like when I sock the sack of flour in Grandma's kitchen.

I peeked around the corner and saw Rudy and Lino standing over the guy on the ground. He looked like the hobo did, but he wasn't dead because I could see puffs of steam coming up from his face when he breathed. Rudy was swaying like he was on a boat. His head was nodding and his hands were stuffed in his pockets.

Lino gave the man on the ground one last kick before Rudy and him left. I lost them in the rows of cars. I stayed pressed against the shed wall and waited for the other man to leave. He took a long time getting up and then he limped away holding his side and disappeared into the night and the fog.

When the men were gone, I ran as fast as I could to Betty's car and got her sweater.

"What happened to you?" she asked me later when we left the show. "You look like you saw a ghost."

"I got lost in the parking lot," I lied, "and couldn't find the car. I guess I got scared."

"Yeah," she said, "you took a long time. I was just praying trouble didn't find you."

I like how she said that—"trouble didn't find you." Lino was trouble. But trouble didn't see me or find me.

16

The light that bounced off her rear-view mirror made Betty's face look red. I heard her mumble, "Damn it. Now what?" Then I heard the siren. Betty slowed down and pulled the car over to the curb. I turned around to look out the back window, but the light was shining in so bright, I couldn't see. Betty fumbled around in her purse.

In a minute a uniform came up next to her side window. I could only see from the belt to the shoulders. Betty rolled the window down.

"Where are you headed?" he asked.

"We're on our way home, Officer." She used that voice she uses when she talks English to the white waitresses at the Woolworth luncheonette.

"Home from where?"

Betty's white voice asked, "Why was I stopped, Officer?"

"Why don't you let me ask the questions?" the cop said. "Do you know how fast you were going?"

"Yes, Officer. I was going twenty in a twenty-five zone. I always drive under the speed limit."

"Oh you do, do you?" I recognized the voice. "License and registration." He leaned down and looked in the window and stared straight at me. He wasn't wearing those sunglasses now, and I could see his eyes squinting in the spotlight. "Is this your kid?"

"No, Officer, he's my nephew." She gave him her license and her registration. I sat sideways looking at Betty who was looking straight out the windshield. We sat like that for a long time. Finally the Turk said, "Step out of the car." I started to reach for the door handle.

"Why did you stop us, Officer?"

"Step out of the car, and go over to the curb, ma'am." The Turk opened the door, and Betty nodded to me to get out.

I got out my side and stood on the curb behind the car. The headlights and the spotlight of the police car were so bright I couldn't see anything around us so I couldn't tell where we were. Betty came over and stood next to me.

"Have a seat," the Turk told us. I looked around.

"I am not sitting on that dirty curb," Betty said.

"Sit down." His voice was hard and mean. Betty smoothed down the back of her dress like ladies do and sat on the curb with her legs kind of slanted to one side. The sides of her white high-heels were going to get scraped on the street. I sat down next to her. The cement was wet and cold.

The Turk walked to his car. He reached in and talked into the microphone of his police radio just like he did on the rightaway. He walked back over to us and shined his flashlight into my face. I looked away.

"I know you." I didn't say anything. "I know you."

I turned back toward him, but I kept my eyes closed and the light turned the insides of my eyelids bright red. The light went off at the same time I heard the snap of the flashlight switch.

"You're one of those kids with the dead tramp. I remember that thing on your face." I still didn't answer him. I almost thought he was going to handcuff me right then and there.

Betty talked in her white voice again. "You still haven't told me why you stopped me."

I heard his boots slap the ground when he walked closer.

"Let me see your car keys."

"They're still in the switch."

The Turk got the keys and snapped on the flashlight again and opened the trunk. He moved things around, then he pulled out the handle of the bumper jack and held it up and shined the light on it, like showing that Betty was hiding it, and he found it. I looked at her. She rolled her eyes and shook her head. He put it back and slammed the trunk shut, then came around to my side and opened the glove compartment and shined his light inside there and under my seat.

The police car radio called him, and he went to answer it. Then he came back and stood in front of Betty. His boots were as shiny as Cruz' fake Florsheims.

"What're you doing on Broadway?" Broadway's an east-west street on the north side of the train tracks.

"Coming home."

"Coming home from where?" Betty didn't answer.

"Why didn't you use Mission Drive or Valley?" Both of these streets were on our side of the tracks, in Sangra.

"It's a free country," Betty said. The Turk moved real close and stood in front of her so his belt buckle was in her face. He stood there so long I could've counted the lace holes of his boots. Then he threw the car keys on top of the trunk. "Next time take Valley." After he said that, he went to his police car and got in and drove away past Betty's car. I watched the taillights until the police car disappeared in the dark.

"Let's get home," Betty told me. I helped her stand up. My butt was cold and itchy. I couldn't wait to get out of there.

The front porch and front room light were on at Grandma's house. Betty didn't turn off the motor.

"What did the Turk mean about taking Valley?" I asked her.

"He means Broadway's for whites and Valley and Mission are for everyone else. I wanted to ask you what he meant about the dead tramp, but it'll have to wait for another time. I promised your dad I'd get you home early." She shook her head. "Do me a favor and don't say anything to your dad about the policeman. It'll only make him mad." I dragged my fingers across my lips to zip them shut. Hush-hush.

Betty leaned over and kissed me on the forehead. I smelled her perfume again. "Thanks for going to the show. I'm glad you were with me when I got stopped."

"Thanks for taking me, Betty." I said. "I had fun." I got out of the car and walked up to the front door. When I turned around to wave goodnight, she was already gone.

In the dream I was lying next to that tee-cat in the parking lot, and my legs were bleeding, but they didn't hurt. I woke up on the couch in the front room, and my underwear was soaked. I got up and stripped the couch without even thinking about it. When I went into the kitchen, my dad was on the phone. I dumped the bed stuff out on the side porch. When I came back in my dad was waiting for me.

"Ted just told me what happened last night. Are you all right?" I wondered what Ted told him.

I asked my dad, "Can I go to the bathroom first?" I went in, but I couldn't pee. I didn't have any left after last night. I got in the shower and stood under the spray trying to think how to answer Dad. I gave up and finished my shower. I put on clean underpants and went back into the kitchen. Dad was sitting at the table. He looked at me and pointed his chin to tell me where to sit. I sat down facing him still in just my underpants.

"Well?"

I started to tell him about the show and Cruz' singing group, but he waved his hand. He wanted to hear about the Turk. I figured Betty already told Ted who called my dad so I spilled the beans. That's when Dad taught me about prejudice.

Well, not really. I already knew what prejudice is. At lunch time, white kids make fun of the tacos we bring from home. They call us wetbacks and greasers and T.J.'s. At the San Gabriel show, the Witch lets us see the first movie, then kicks us out.

And people say things to me about my port-wine stain too. Grown-ups stare at me and kids call me "matchhead" and "scarface" when they point at my birthmark. Dad told me things I already knew, but I didn't know it was called prejudice.

I went back to the front room to get clothes to wear. Rudy's door was closed. I didn't remember hearing him come in last night. I looked back to see if Dad was still in the kitchen. He wasn't. I knocked soft on the door. I waited for a time and knocked again. I opened it real slow.

Light was coming through the open blinds. I could see everything in the room. The bed was made, and there was an open empty suitcase on top of it. I went out and closed the door behind me.

I went in the kitchen and made myself a mean Sam sandwich and poured some Valley Fresh in my school thermos. I put the sandwich and the thermos in my school lunchbox and went up to the club. It was Sunday. I knew I should go to church with Grandma and Mom, but I didn't have to serve Mass, and I had too much to think about to talk to God. I sat on the cardboard and chewed on the sandwich, but it didn't feel good in my mouth. I swallowed without tasting. And the milk tasted sour like it always does when you drink it out of a thermos.

"Was I all right?" I thought about my dad's question, and I felt like what Rudy must feel like. Wherever he was, he must've felt like the Turk knew him and had an eye on him and was waiting for just the right time to arrest him and send him back to prison.

I've seen pictures of the war in Italy in *Life* magazine at the school library and I've seen war movies. I thought about Rudy fighting in the war.

In the movies, you don't see people really die. They just fall down when they get shot. And the good guys never get hurt. They don't even get dirty. I thought about Ted's burns and his Purple Heart. I got asco, and I didn't know if it was because the ham was bad or the milk was old, but I wanted to lean over the edge of the roof and throw up. The club didn't feel good all alone, and I wanted to get down and find Danny and Marco and Little so we could be together when the Turk came for us.

I put the rest of my sandwich back in the lunch box and poured out the milk and watched it hit the ground in a white splash. Then I put the thermos in the lunchbox and climbed down the rusty fence.

When I got to the kitchen, Rudy was at the sink.

"Hi, Rudy." He turned around. He was holding a glass of water.

"Ey, Liddo Man." He looked tired and sick.

"I haven't seen you around. Where you been?"

"Oh, here and there." He shook his shoulders and leaned back on the sink. "When do you start school, kid?"

I put my lunchbox on the counter next to him. "I already started," I said. "We went back right after Labor Day." I wanted to wash the fence rust off my hands, but he was standing in the way. When he figured that out, he moved to the side so I could use the sink.

"Right," he said like he knew that, only he forgot. I washed my hands and wiped them on a dishrag.

"Rudy, can you do me a favor? Can you call me Manuel or Manny? Call me Man if you want. Just don't call me Little Man."

Rudy gulped a drink of water, put his glass in the sink, and leaned on the counter.

"My friends call me Man, like in Man-on-Fire, because of my birthmark. Call me Man, okay?"

"*Ey*, that's pretty good. Man-on-Fire. That's a righteous *placa*."

"What's a *placa*?"

"That's another habit I got to kick," he said. "A *placa*'s a nickname. We use a lot of nicknames in the *pinta*. In the joint." He chuckled. "In prison."

He caught me staring at his red knuckles. He put his hands in his pockets.

"*Ey*, Man-on-Fire," he said real quick and happy, like he just got a good idea. "You got time to talk? We got to get to know each other, you know? We got to catch up." Rudy had a funny way of talking, kind of sing-songy and chipping the ends off his words.

Rudy put his arm around my shoulders and steered me out

to the porch. I sat down on the hobo chair, but then I got up so Rudy could sit there. He put his hand on my shoulder and leaned on the little porch wall and crossed his arms.

"So, you got a *ruca* or what?"

I like Kiko Yamanaka, but she's not my girlfriend. "Nah."

"I had a girlfriend in seventh grade," he said. "A *gabachita*. Her name was Inga Lindstrom." He smiled to remember. "She was like a white girl, you know?"

He got quiet and looked past me at the screen door. I turned around to see who he was talking to, but there wasn't anybody there. "She had blond hair and light-blue eyes. And *pecas*, freckles on her nose.

"Well, she wasn't actually my girlfriend." He said *actually* like *ack-chully*. "We didn't go out on no dates or nothing, you know? We just kind of hung around together for seventh grade. She couldn't never be like my real girlfriend, you know? Because she's *gabacha* and I'm *Chicano*. But we used to hold hands in the cafeteria and out in the yard. And once in a while when we were by ourselves, we would kiss. That's all we did was kiss a couple of times."

He stopped talking. I waited to see if he would say some more.

"That was a long time ago. And the last time I seen you, you was what, two years old?"

"I think I was four," I said. "But I don't remember much."

I wanted to know so much about him. I wanted to hear his side of the story Grandma and Cruz told me, but I was scared he would get mad or something so I sat there and didn't say nothing.

Y ou play baseball?" Rudy asked me. His voice made me jump a little.

"Little League."

"Oh, yeah?" Rudy smiled. "I love baseball. When I was a kid, I played wherever there was a game. Pretty good outfielder. What do you play?"

"Second base."

"You any good?"

I wiggled my shoulders. "All glove, no bat."

Rudy nodded. "Your dad could pitch swift. He could've been in the big leagues, you know? Like Raul Valdez."

He stopped talking and looked down.

I decided to take a chance.

"What happened, Uncle Rudy—Rudy? Why did you go to prison?"

He laughed a little sad laugh and shook his head. A part of me was sorry I asked him. He looked up at me then he turned and looked at the mountains so all I could see was the back of him. Then he pointed at Mount Wilson.

"Do you see that heart with the arrow through it?" he said.

I was shocked. I thought I was the only one who saw the heart. Nobody else ever said anything about it.

"You see it too?" I asked him. I got up and stood next to him.

"Oh, yeah. It looks just like a heart with a arrow going through it. Can I tell you something?"

"Sure."

"Whenever I look at that mountain it reminds me how many times I broke my mother's heart. That's the worst part of things. That's what I hate the most about my life. All my life. Everything bad I ever did. Like that arrow going right through her heart."

He was talking to the mountain. He had his hands in his pockets. Then he took them out and put them on the top of the wall in front of him so he could look at the backs. The knuckles were puffy and red. He went over and sat down in the hobo chair. He looked tired now.

"Sometimes I wished I was never born. For your grandma, you know? Like if I wasn't born, her life would be happy." He shut his eyes. "I don't want you to do this or anything, okay? Don't even think about doing it. Just because I told you. It's not no way to solve your problems, so don't try it, *me entiendes*?"

I didn't know what he was talking about.

He started talking real slow like you do when you're not sure if you should say what you're going to say. "One time when things were going real bad, I went out to the tracks and stood there between the rails. I wanted the train to just hit me and take away all the trouble I made. I thought about it, what it would feel like, you know? When the train hit me? I thought it would hurt like hell for like a split second, then no more pain, you know? Maybe it would be like drowning. I wanted to drown myself on those tracks just to stop giving pain to the people I love. But I didn't have the guts."

He stopped talking again. By this time I was sitting on the arm of the hobo chair. I wasn't looking at him. We were both looking at the broken-hearted mountain.

"I hated the way my mother would have to go to court to beg one judge after another to give me another chance. Then when I would get the chance, I would jack it up and go back to juvvie. I thought when the judge made me choose between the service or the joint, I could finally make my family proud of me. So I enlisted in the Marines."

I was surprised about the Marines. Cruz said Rudy was in the army like Dad.

"You were in the Marines?"

"First Marine Provisionals. *Semper Fi.*" He smiled but it didn't last long. "Even that went wrong. Right after boot camp, our outfit got sent to Algeria in North Africa. That place is like the Mojave Desert. Your dad ever take you to the Mojave?"

I shook my head.

"Ask him to take you there sometimes. It's different than the Arizona desert when we were liddo kids."

I always thought Africa was pure jungle like the Tarzan movies.

"We seen some righteous action along the north coast of Africa. This is the bad part. I don't know if I should tell you, you know? Being that you're a little kid and all. But then your dad probably already told you about other bad things I did. But before I tell you, I want you to think of something first.

"See that wounded heart up there on the mountain? The

funny thing is, if you go to Alhambra or El Monte and look at the mountain from there you don't see no heart. What you see is a small mountain in front of a bigger mountain. There's no wounded heart if you look at it from a different angle. They're just mountains. It's only from here that they look like they do, you know?"

I promised myself I'd try to remember to look at it from Alhambra the next time I was there.

"Okay, well, I'm going to tell you something not even your dad knows. You don't have to keep it a secret, but you don't have to go telling the whole world either, *me entiendes*?"

"Yeah."

"There's this little town on the Algeria coast called Arzeu. It's even smaller than San Gabriel. About the size of Sangra. Just a little port town on the sea. Well, we have to take it to get to a bigger city called Oran.

"We take Arzeu pretty easy, you know? So we're on our way out of town towards Oran, eight of us in the bed of a deuce-and-a-half. I'm sitting with my back against the headboard next to Jimmy Beane. I'll never forget him. He was this cracker kid from Alabama. A farm kid a year younger than me. He lied about his age to get in the Marines.

He hated the farm and the 'Corps was his way out. Just a farm boy from Alabama who didn't know enough about Mexicans to be prejudice. He though I was Italian. He would say it like 'Eye-talian.' He called me '*Dolfo*' and I called him '*Frijol*,' you know? I tried to teach him about Mexicans but I couldn't get it through to him that I wasn't Italian. He kept saying when we get to Italy, I should tell him which ones was my kin so he wouldn't shoot them.

"I'm tired and sleepy so I don't really know what happened, you know? But sudden-like, I hear a boom and the truck bumps up and down, sudden-like and real hard, and then the deuce-and-a-half starts tipping over. I'm sliding off and everything is happening in slow motion. I can feel my ass sliding along the floorboards, and then I guess I black out because the next thing I remember I'm on my hands and knees in the middle of some dry weeds and hot sand. My helmet is off, and my head hurts, and my ears are ringing.

"I look around and see the truck all upside down in a ditch next to the road. The front tires are spinning slow and black smoke is coming from underneath. Then I see my squad. There's bodies scattered everywhere. I check to see if I'm bleeding. I don't see no blood, but my ears are ringing and my head's pounding it hurts so bad.

"I get up and try to run to the closest man. He's face down on the dirt road. My legs don't work good, but I do the best I can to get to him. It's this guy named Gentry. All I know about him is he's a white guy—a lance corporal—and he's from Fresno. I roll him on his back and he's choking and his face is a bloody mess. I put my fingers in his mouth and pull out his tongue and a bunch of broken teeth. He's moaning real bad, but I don't know what I can do for him. I go to another guy who's facedown in the ditch. He isn't moving. When I get to him and turn him over, it's Jimmy Beane. When I see him, I throw up all over him. I guess the deuce-and-a-half must've rolled on him because his head's crushed and he's covered in blood. All I can think to do is hold his hand."

Rudy stopped talking for a long time. He made a sound in his throat like he was choking. I didn't know what I should do. Then he started talking again. When he did, his voice was different. Like somebody was squeezing his neck. He took out a handkerchief from his back pocket and wiped his nose.

"I been in fights and I seen guys get beat up pretty bad, and I even seen guys die, and I did my share of killing in a couple of fire-fights, but I never lost a buddy or seen anything like what happened to Jimmy Beane. I sat there in the ditch holding his hand for I don't know how long.

"Then he says something. I don't see how he could talk with his head smashed up so bad, but he says something to me. I can't understand him so I lean down and put my ear right next to his mouth. I could hear the blood gurgle when he breathes in. 'Hurts,' he says. 'Shoot me,' he says. I could feel his hand try to squeeze mine. The blood gurgles. 'Hurts.'"

Rudy stopped again and put the handkerchief over his eyes.

"When I re-lize what he wants, I don't want to do what he's asking me, but I could see he's hurt so bad. And he's crying. I sit up, and I could hear him hiss the words 'hurt' and 'shoot' over and over. I stand up and put the muzzle of my M-1 against his head. I hear him hiss something, and I close my eyes and squeeze the trigger."

Rudy gave a deep, croaky cough into the handkerchief, and his shoulders jumped up and down. After a long time, they settled down like earthquakes do. He took the handkerchief down from his eyes, and they were red. They didn't look at me but past me at the mountain.

"I sit down next to Jimmy Beane for a long time. Then I turn the rifle around and put the muzzle in my mouth. I want to pull the trigger again. I want to be with him. To pay for everything, you know? For all the bad things I done my whole life. But I don't have the guts. Why did he had to be the one to die, you know? After all, he was a innocent kid. I should've died, not him. I deserve it way more than him, you know?

"Then another unit comes along and finds us. They put us all in the bed of another deuce, and I sit next to Jimmy Beane all the way to the field hospital. They split us up and check me out, and I guess I'm okay because a few days later I get orders assigning me to another unit headed for Italy. But I'm no good to fight no more. I wait for them to charge me with killing Jimmy, but they never do. All they do is send me home and let me go with a general discharge which isn't much better than a dishonorable."

Rudy kept sniffing because his nose was running. He used the handkerchief and looked down at the floor and kept shaking his head like saying no. I wanted to do something to make him feel better, but then I remembered what happened to Little. We were playing at his house one time when we saw a dog get hit by a car. The dog looked hurt bad and kept trying to get up. When Little tried to pick the dog up, it bit him. I didn't know how to help Rudy so I just sat on the floor with my back against the porch wall and waited for him to come back.

"I done a lot of bad things in my life. I know I hurt my 'ama and my 'apa and the familia real bad. I guess I'm what they call bad seed. I just wish I knew why God even put me on this earth, you know?" He looked at me. "No, you don't know. I only been here a little while, but I already know you're good seed like your daddy. He doesn't want you near me because he's afraid you might catch what I have like they catch polio or something. But you're not like me. You won't catch nothing bad from me." He wiped his eyes and blew his nose in the handkerchief. "I guess your uncle Rudy's just a big cry baby, huh?" he said. He looked around and looked surprised that he was on the front porch. He stood up and put the handkerchief back in his back pocket. He leaned over and mussed up my hair.

"Don't tell nobody about the crying, okay, Man?" I nodded and watched him go in through the screen door. I watched the door till the front door closed behind it.

18

All I could think about was the story Rudy told me. What would it be like to see Danny or Marco or Little dying and me not able to keep them alive? It seems like it would hurt more to see a friend suffering than to be the one dying, but I don't know and I don't want to know.

I thought about Rudy and how hard it must be for him to live outside of prison. Everywhere he looked, he found trouble. And now that he was on parole, trouble came looking for him—like that guy Lino.

He was trouble. I wish Rudy would've stayed away from him.

I already told you I don't want to go to high school. The seventh grade is the second-to-last stop before that.

One day Capone told us we set a record for the hottest day for that date in history. She seemed happy about that and showed us the thermometer she keeps on the wall outside our classroom. It said one hundred and ten degrees. I sat in my desk and begged God to make the day go fast so I could go cool off up in the club.

When I got home I could hardly wait to wash up and change. But when I went in the kitchen my dad was standing at the telephone talking to somebody. He put his hand over the talking part and jerked his head to the side for me to get lost.

When I came out of the bathroom, I went through the kitchen as slow as I could to hear what dad was saying. He was talking Spanish. It sounded like he was either talking to Rudy or about him. And his voice was real rough. I heard him say, "Okay, but it's going to take some time."

I went over and sat in front of the TV. When my dad came in, I asked him why he was home. He told me, "Never mind." He went into his room and was there for a little while. Then he came out wearing clean clothes.

I asked him, "Can I go with you?"

"No," he growled.

He went out the kitchen door, pulled the car out of the driveway and drove away like he was in a hurry. When I went in the kitchen, Grandma was at the stove moving pots and pans around. I looked at the clock. It was too early to start supper. She wasn't even cleaning any beans. I walked up next to her. She was crying.

"Grandma, what's the matter?" She turned then and hugged me real tight.

"*Mijo,* oh, *mijo.*" I could feel her chest shaking.

"What's wrong, Grandma?"

"Oh, Rodolfo, you have broken my mother's heart!" It was weird to hear Rudy's name in Spanish. She only says my name in Spanish like that when she's mad. But she didn't sound mad at Rudy. I stood there and let her hold me. Pretty soon her bony chest stopped shaking. She let me go. "We have to say the rosary, *mijito*. For your *tío*."

We went into her room and stood in front of the santos. "We have to pray to Saint Peter and Saint Paul because they both were in prison." I kneeled down next to Grandma's bed. I looked in the case for the statues of Peter and Paul. Peter's an old guy holding a set of keys. Paul is the one with a book in one hand and a sword in the other. I found Peter standing behind St. Therese looking over the Little Flower's shoulder. And I spotted Paul standing next to San Judas, the apostle with the flame sticking out the top of his head. Paul was turned like he's looking out the window and wishing he was anywhere else but in that crowded case.

I could say the rosary in Spanish and think about other things at the same time. I thought about Rudy. Then I thought about what happened at the Legion. Then I thought about the hobo. I always ended up thinking about the hobo. About halfway through the rosary, Dorothy came in. She kneeled down on the other side of Grandma and said the rest of the rosary with us.

When we finished, I asked Grandma what was the matter, but she just shook her head and told me to go do my homework.

"Is Rudy dead?" I asked. Grandma laughed a little nervous laugh, but her face didn't look like I said something funny. I heard a car pull up in front of the house. I went to the screen door. It was Ted's car. Betty was driving, and Mom was in the passenger side. I ran out to meet them.

"Mom, what happened? Grandma's crying and Dad came home from work early and left."

Mom kissed the top of my head real fast and rushed into the house. Betty wasn't smiling. She scratched the back of my head soft-like while we walked inside.

Mom was holding Grandma in her arms and Grandma was crying again. Betty pushed me toward the front room where Dorothy was.

"Watch TV. I'll bring your supper later. Just stay in here, okay?"

I didn't really pay attention to the outer-space movie that was on after the cartoon hour ended, and I didn't taste my supper. I spent the whole time trying to hear what the grown-ups were saying in the kitchen. Finally Betty came in and turned off the TV.

"Your uncle Rudy is in the hospital. He's in pretty bad shape. Your father's at the hospital with him."

"What happened to him?"

She shook her head. "All I know is he's pretty bad." I didn't know if she meant he was hurt bad or that he was a bad person. "Get your school clothes ready for tomorrow in case you have to sleep over my house, okay?" She mussed up my hair, but this time I could tell she wasn't playing. She gave Dorothy a kiss on her head and went back to the kitchen.

I found out later that Dad spent the night at the hospital, then came home and changed and went straight to work. We didn't have to sleep at Betty's. I'm glad because when I woke up the next day, my sheets were soaked.

Rudy was hurt real bad, and Dad was mad at him, and Grandma's heart was broken, and I was a pee baby.

I took a shower and got dressed, then I took my sheets out to the cuartito. When I came back inside, Betty was in the kitchen with Mom and Grandma.

"Betty's going to drop you off at school," Mom told me, "and then take me into work. So eat your breakfast, and don't waste time." Dorothy was already dressed. Her hair was brushed, and she was halfway done with her cereal. Grandma was still in her nightgown and robe, and her hair was still in that braid she wears to bed. She looked tired and real old. She was holding her rosary.

I was out in the playground at lunchtime with Danny and Marco and Little when I found out what happened to Rudy. Cruz told me from the other side of the fence where he was hanging out with Big and the other guys. He waved for me to come over.

"Did you hear about Rudy?" I stood there waiting for him to tell me. "Well, did you?"

"My dad didn't come home last night. And I know Rudy got hurt."

Cruz turned to his friends. "Dumb ass. Rudy got his ass kicked by the Turk." Then him and his friends laughed. "He busted him at Smith Park and beat the piss out of him." They laughed again.

I told Cruz, "I don't think that's funny."

"Who cares what you think, pee baby?"

My whole body started burning. I wanted to take off my shirt and run so the wind would cool me off. I knew if I stayed there he would tell everybody there that I was twelve, and I still wet my bed. Pretty soon everybody in the high school and then in the grammar school would know.

Before I could do anything, Danny pulled my arm and turned me around. "Let's go." Marco and Danny and Little walked me away from the fence. I could hear the teenagers laughing. Maybe everybody knew already.

I couldn't think about schoolwork the rest of the day. Me and the gang walked home without talking. When they dropped me off, Marco said, "Those guys are stupid. Don't pay attention to them."

"See you tomorrow at school," Danny said. He patted me on the shoulder.

I dropped my book bag in the kitchen and went to lay down on the couch. Grandma's salón was cool and dark. I was sweating and had a headache that was splitting my head like a sandía. I thought about Rudy getting beat up. I remembered his hands the day we were in the kitchen. I wondered if he got beat up the same way him and Marcel beat up that guy at the Legion.

The next thing I knew Grandma was shaking my arm. "Wake up, mijito," I heard her say. "Wash your face and change your clothes. Your daddy's going to take us to see Rudy."

"What about Dorothy?" I asked her.

"Betulia already picked her up."

I checked that my pants were dry. I took off my shirt and pulled a clean one out of the clothes box. I was finishing buttoning it up when Dad honked. Grandma walked fast through the front room like she was a younger woman.

"Come on, mijito."

After a while driving, Dad turned into the parking lot of a huge grey building and parked.

"Where are we?"

"General Hospital. This is where they brought Rudy."

19

"Why didn't they take him to Valley Hospital?" Valley Hospital was just across the tracks from our neighborhood on Broadway. It's where I was born. Dad didn't say anything.

I waited on a bench with Grandma while Dad talked to a lady at the entrance counter. Dad came back to us.

"Tenth floor."

We followed a blue line painted on the floor and got in that elevator with another family. The mom was holding a crying baby. She seemed as old and tired as Grandma. She kept putting a *chupón* in the baby's mouth, and the baby kept spitting it out. Three other kids were with her, and they all wore old clothes. Their skin was kind of dirty brown, like coffee with not enough milk. The girl looked about as old as Dorothy but way littler than Dorothy. She stared at me and the shiny darks of her eyes were like black olives. I watched her olives follow the shape of my port-wine stain. She got to my red hair, then she looked at my eyes. When I smiled at her, she hid her face in her mother's dress.

The littlest kid had a runny nose and his *mocos* were like thick clear water on his top lip. I got asco and I had to turn away and look up at the numbers over the door.

The "10" lit up and the operator opened the elevator doors. We stepped out into the middle of a long hallway. The big sign on the wall in front of us said, "Medical Detention Unit. Los Angeles County Sheriff."

On one side of the hallway people were sitting on beat-up steel chairs or standing up leaning against the walls. Little kids were sitting on the floor and running up and down the hall. All the people were Mexicans or *negros*. One end of the hall was blocked by steel bars. An old Mexican man was talking to a policeman on the other side of the bars. He was holding a white cowboy hat like men from Mexico wear.

"Wait right here," Dad told me and Grandma. He went to the bars and stood behind the Mexican man. The bell rang again and the elevator doors opened. Me and Grandma had to move out of the way to let another family come out of the elevator.

A *negro* man got up from a chair and offered it to Grandma. She smiled and said, "No, thank you." But before the man could sit back down, a woman who just got off the elevator ran to the chair and plopped herself down in it. Grandma and the man looked at each other and just shook their heads.

Dad came back over to where we were. He looked so different from the other men there in the hall. He looked like a white man compared to them. His skin was lighter. The clothes he wore fit him.

"Maldonado." Our name was called even though people were there before us. The voice sounded like a dog bark. Dad touched my shoulder, and we walked over to the wall of bars. The bar-door opened with a clank, and we walked through. A different policeman on the other side told us to empty our pockets in a steel tray on a wood table. Dad put in his wallet and car keys and pack of Camels and his Zippo lighter Mom gave him one Father's Day. Grandma put in her purse. I took out my handkerchief, a pack of Juicy Fruit gum, and a baseball card I wanted to give Rudy. The officer looked through the things on the tray. He opened Grandma's purse and emptied it in the tray and looked at what she had, then he told her to put it back in her purse. The same with Dad's stuff. He pointed at my things, and I picked them up and stuffed them back in my pockets. "Six," he barked at my dad.

We found Room Six and went in. Four men in four beds. Rudy was by the window. His head was wrapped in bandages and both his eyes were bloodshot and black. His lips were puffed up and purple. He looked asleep, but when Dad got to his bed, he opened his eyes.

"*Traje a 'amá para verte,*" Dad grumbled. Then he moved over and stood looking out the window. I stood behind Grandma and watched her start crying again. She blessed Rudy on the forehead and chest and said "*Ay, mijo,*" over and over. She kissed his cheeks and wiped her tears off his face. Then she kissed his hands and pressed them against her cheek.

I looked at Dad. He kept staring out the window like something important was happening outside. Grandma whispered things to Rudy in Spanish. Then she stopped and moved to the side and said, "Manuelito's here too." I never heard her call me that way before. I moved closer to the bed and smiled the best I could to Rudy.

I pulled the baseball card out of my pocket. It was all bent and folded from getting stuffed in my pocket. I smoothed out the card the best I could and held up it so he could see it, and then I laid it on the little table next to his bed.

"I didn't have no holy cards," I told him, "so I brought you one of my favorite baseball cards, okay? It's my Bobby Avila. Sorry it's all bent up."

He smiled at me the best he could and said, "Thanks, Man. He's my favorite too." Rudy's voice sounded all scratchy like an old man. I didn't know what to say so I told him, "I hope you get well fast."

Then I went over to the window next to Dad. I wanted to see what he was looking at. When Dad felt me next to him, he looked down at me, then at Grandma. He said, "I'll wait outside." He didn't even say goodbye to Rudy. He just walked out of the room.

Something told me to go with him, so I waved bye at Rudy and told him, "See you soon." I left him there with Grandma.

Dad was leaning on the wall and looking at the floor when I came out. He saw me and stood up straight. He asked me, "Is your Grandma ready to go?" I shook my head to tell him no.

I asked him, "How come you didn't talk to Rudy, Dad?"

"I don't have anything to say to him."

"Are you mad because he got arrested or because he got beat up?" He didn't answer me. We stood there for like half an hour until Grandma came out and closed the door so it didn't make noise. She walked past Dad to the steel bar door without looking at him.

Nobody talked on the way home until we got to Alhambra. Then Grandma turned her body toward Dad. She started speaking Spanish fast, but I was able to get most of it. "You should've talked to him. He's your brother. He'll always be your brother whether you like it or not."

Dad reminded me of me when Mom scolds me. He stared straight ahead with his hands on the steering wheel. He didn't say anything back. Grandma kept on scolding him. "You promised me when your father died you would look after him." When Dad didn't answer, Grandma stopped talking and turned her body back to the front. She went the rest of the way home looking out the side window.

Saturday's the day my dad washes the car. When I went outside after breakfast, Dad was in the driveway under the ramada with a cigarette in one hand and the hose in the other spraying soap off the hood of the Chevy. I waited on the side porch until he turned off the faucet.

"Do you hate Rudy?" I'd been wanting to ask him that for a long time.

He spun around to me, and his eyes were really big. I guess I surprised him. He took a big puff of his Camel. He blew white smoke up at the ramada and picked a piece of tobacco off the tip of his tongue. "What makes you think I hate Rudy?" he asked me.

"You didn't talk to him at the hospital. And Grandma was mad at you."

He was quiet for a minute. Then he grabbed the chamois and started pushing it around to get the water off the car.

"I don't hate him. Your uncle did some bad things. He broke promises to your grandma. He hurt and shamed the family. I'm mad at him, but I don't hate him."

"What did he do?"

Dad stopped wiping the car. He put the chamois down and turned to lean against the Chevy. He threw his cigarette into the soap bucket. "Manny, what do you know about your uncle?"

That was easy. "He's your little brother. He went to high school, but he didn't graduate. He joined the Marines and was in the war. He killed his buddy and…"

"What?"

"Rudy told me he killed his Marine buddy Beans."

Dad squatted down so we could be eye to eye.

"What do you mean he killed his buddy?" His blue eyes were the color of the sky and there were tiny red veins on his nose.

"We talked about stuff one day. I don't remember when. He told me their truck got blew up, and Beans got hurt bad and was telling Rudy to kill him, and Rudy shot him in the head."

"Beans?"

"That's his name. Beans. He was his Marine buddy from Georgia or someplace. Rudy said the truck crushed him, and he was hurt so bad Beans asked Rudy to take away his pain. Rudy didn't want to, but Beans kept telling him it hurt so bad. And there was no doctors around or nothing. It was just him and Beans. So Rudy shot him in his head and Beans died. Rudy said everything changed after that. He didn't want to be a Marine any more. He has nightmares about Beans all the time. He said he wishes he died instead of Beans."

My dad put his hand on my shoulder.

"Dad, what's going to happen to Rudy?"

"Rudy was using drugs," he said. "He broke the law and so he has to go back to prison when he gets out of the hospital."

"But why is he in the hospital instead of jail?" Dad stood up and started to coil up the hose. He stopped suddenly and looked straight at me.

"Turkness." He didn't have to say no more for me to get it.

"But Dad, can the Turk do that?"

"The Turk can do whatever he wants in this neighborhood."

"But why do they let him?" I guess Dad didn't hear me because he started coiling the hose again like I wasn't even there. When he didn't answer me, I went back inside.

Little's usually my partner when we serve at Thursday night rosary and benediction. Dad drops us off at the Mission and Little's mom or Big picks us up after. Once in a while when Little doesn't show up and I serve alone, I walk to Betty's after so Ted can bring me home.

This was one of those times. To get to Betty's, I have to walk down Mission Drive and then back up to Sunset. That's about eight blocks. Or I can take the shortcut through Smith Park. I did that a few times, and I always hope I don't run into the tee-cats. They usually hang out by the snack bar on the other side of the swimming pool so I stay away from that part of the park.

This time the park was empty. The only light on was next to the tennis court gate. All I could see in the light was the old drinking fountain that's always busted. I walked by the tennis courts and the fountain and then past the handball courts and crossed the street to the old train station.

Way before I was born, the train used to stop in San Gabriel. That was back when there was the Mission Play which the whole world came to see because it told about the early Spanish mission days in California. But when they stopped showing it, nobody got off the train in San Gabriel anymore so they closed the station.

So now the San Gabriel station is just two locked buildings—a passenger hall with the windows painted so you can't see inside and a baggage building with a wood platform and a ramp.

I was almost past the passenger hall when I heard a sound I'd heard once before. I stopped and listened harder. It was the sound of somebody getting beat up, and it was coming from inside. I hid in the shadows. I was scared and sorry I took the shortcut. It was cold now, and I wanted to close up my jacket, but I knew it would make that zipping noise so I left it open.

I leaned against the wall and waited for the sound to stop. But this time the beating went on a lot longer than at the Legion when Rudy and Marcel beat up that other tee-cat.

I heard punches and kicks and the voice of a boy crying. A man's hard voice told him to shut up and called the boy dirty names and "nigger."

The boy cried and cried, and then he started moaning and then he was quiet, but the kicking didn't stop. I wanted to cry too. I wanted to be home. I wanted to wake up in my pee, and find out I was just dreaming because it was so bad how the boy was getting beat up.

The punching and kicking stopped. I heard footsteps coming toward me. I pushed myself into the wall where it was the darkest. A shadow passed by me walking fast and breathing hard. Even though it was dark, I could see who it was. The shadow turned to look back, and I thought he saw me, but then he walked into the night and in a minute I heard a car start up and burn rubber and drive away fast. I waited.

The hall was so quiet I could hear my own heart pounding. I looked around, and then I went to the door. It was open and the chain that kept it locked was hanging from one of the handles like a dead snake.

I peeked my head inside. I couldn't see anything at first, but I could smell B.O. and the stink of poop. When my eyes got used to the dark, I could see a body laying on the floor next to a tipped-over bench. There was a round puddle of shiny, black water around his head like those halos on Grandma's santos. The body was laying on his back like he was just looking at the stars.

When I got up close to him, he looked bigger than a boy but not a man. He looked like Lawrence Collison, but I wasn't sure because his face was all puffed up and covered with blood. One eye was swelled shut, and his mouth was a black hole.

I didn't want to, but I put my ear next to his mouth. He wasn't breathing. I put my hand on his chest. It felt bony and warm, but I couldn't feel his heartbeat. The smell of B.O. and poop and blood was bad, and I ran out of the passenger hall and threw up on the cement, and I didn't care who heard me. I ran away from that station and didn't stop running till I got to Betty's.

My dad got to Betty's fast after Ted called him on the phone. I was sitting in the parlor drinking a glass of sugar water Betty gave me for my nerves when he came in. I stood up, but I was still shaking.

"What the hell were you doing at the station at night?" Dad's face was red, and his voice sounded hard like it did when he chewed out Rudy on the front porch. He stomped up close to me like he was going to give me a belt whipping.

Betty stood next to me. "Calm down, Manuel. Can't you see he's already a nervous wreck?" She put her hand on my shoulder. I looked down at the floor and waited for the sound of him pulling off his belt.

"How many times have I told you to stay away from there?" Dad's face was right over me, and his breath was hot on the top of my head. "You don't have any business going there at night!"

"I was just taking a short cut," I whispered to the floor. Dad's shoes were almost touching mine like Danny's did in the caboose. "Little didn't show up to serve with me, and I had to walk here. The park's a short cut." I kept talking so I wouldn't cry.

Ted came out of the kitchen carrying a cup of coffee.

I felt Dad back off from me. Betty made me sit down in Ted's easy chair, but she still stood over me like she was protecting me from Dad. Ted put the cup on the table next to the couch. I guess Dad got the message because he went to the couch and sat down. Ted leaned against the tile fireplace and crossed his arms. When I looked at Dad he was staring hard at me, so I dropped my eyes to the rug in front of me.

"What do you want to do, Manuel?" Ted asked.

"Do we call the police?" Dad said.

"And say what?"

Dad was quiet a long time. "I see what you mean," he said finally. "They're going to want to know what Manny was doing there."

Betty's voice made me jump. "You don't think the police are going to say Manny did that to the Collison boy?"

"Can't I just tell the truth?" I asked.

Ted answered for Dad. "You don't know the truth. Not all of it. And they'll want it all."

"But I do know it all!"

"Unless you know who beat up Lawrence, you don't."

Dad got up off the couch. "Come on, then. It's late and you have school tomorrow."

"You're not going to make him go to school, are you?" Betty said. "After what he's just gone through and the state he's in?"

"We'll see," Dad grunted.

We didn't talk in the car on the way home. I sat looking out at the sleeping neighborhood through the side window. We passed Silverman's and Big's house. Both of them were dark. When we got home, Grandma didn't talk about what happened. Neither did Mom. She just made me take a shower and go right to bed.

I laid under the covers of the couch, but I couldn't fall asleep, so I waited until Mom and Dad's bedroom door closed and everybody was in bed. Then I got up and went to the front door and opened it. I stood there listening to the night through the screen door. The neighborhood was quiet except for some barking that was probably Cerberus, Louie Mora's big, black dog from down the street who always tries to bite anybody that goes by his yard.

I felt like time was spinning backwards, taking me back to the day when we found the hobo. After my confession to Father Simon, I was good with God, but time and the Turk weren't going to let me slide with the law. I listened for a siren that would come to take me. Not to jail, but to the shutdown train station. The Turk was going to make me say I killed the hobo. And he was going to keep asking me if I knew who killed Lawrence Collison. He would even beat me up like he beat up Rudy until I told him. But when I told him, he would kill me too.

I heard the horn of the SP engine coming on an east current.

It was probably passing the Mission. In a minute it would be rumbling past my house. I went back to the couch and pulled my blanket over me. I thought about what Rudy told me about drowning himself on the track so he could end the trouble. I wonder what it felt like to drown. I think I fell asleep just before the train came past and the house shook like a baby earthquake.

21

I guess Mom and Dad took Betty's advice because Grandma kept me home from school. I spent Friday sitting in the front room staring out the screen door at the mountains. There was nothing on TV but soap operas and "Queen for a Day," and Grandma wouldn't let me go outside. There was nobody to play with either. I watched six trains go by in the morning. Four were on a west current and two were headed east.

I took a nap after lunch, but I couldn't really sleep because all I could think of was what I saw last night and what was going to happen. I must've fell asleep though because I jumped when I heard meowing at the screen door.

I flipped the hook off the latch.

"Are you sick?"

Danny was still in his school clothes, and his blue school shirt had a dark brown spot next to the pocket.

I shook my head.

"Nah, Grandma kept me home. Did I miss Dice Cream day?"

Dice Cream day is really Gabriel's Day. St. Gabriel the Archangel is the patron saint of our mission and school and even our city. Once a year on Gabriel's Day, there's Mass and schoolwork in the morning. But from lunch time to the end of school is a play day. The cafeteria people give out Hawaiian Punch and those squares of ice cream called Dice Cream. Danny must've had a chocolate one.

"Yeah," he said. "I was going to bring you one when you weren't in school, but it would've melted. Sorry. So, how come you skipped school?"

I thought about how I was going to tell him. I said, "Let's go up to the club."

When we were up there laying down and looking at the sky, Danny said, "I haven't been to the club since school started." Everything was the way we left it the last time, except the cardboard we put on top of the pallets was crinkly and dark brown from a rain in August.

"So, how come you stayed home today?" Danny got up and walked to the edge of the roof on top of Yoci's bathroom and stood there looking down.

"Hey, get away from there," I told him. "You want to get me in more trouble?"

Danny came back to the pallet. He reached up and pulled an avocado off a low branch. It was all shriveled up and black like Tanaka's finger. He threw it. It smacked down on Grandpa's driveway. "So?" he asked me again.

"My dad made me." Then I told him about Lawrence Collison.

"Oh, God, Man!" he said. "What are you going to do?"

I told him my dad was going to talk to some lawyer. I told him I was scared. I told him about drowning on the tracks.

"You can't do that," he said. "Suicide's a sin. You'll go straight to hey-yell!"

I knew I couldn't drown myself. Hell was bad, but I didn't want to do that to Dad and Mom and Grandma and Dorothy. I moved, and I felt the cardboard crunch under my back. Danny was sitting next to me now. He had his knees pulled up to his chin, and he was staring straight ahead.

"Are you sure it was the Turk?" he asked me.

I lifted up off my back and held myself up on my elbows and didn't say nothing. There I was on a refrigerator box on top of a wood pallet with my best friend. But it was really like I was on a raft floating on a river of trouble. I couldn't get off and I couldn't steer. I just had to go where the current took me like those people on the Sunset Limited. But at least they knew where they were going. I didn't know where this river was taking me.

"What are you thinking about, Man?" Danny asked me. I wanted to say something, but all the things in my mind were spinning around, and I couldn't grab an idea to save my life. I shook my head.

Danny said, "That Turk is a mean son-of-a-bitch." He didn't look at me. He was watching his fingernail peel a scab off his elbow. "That's what my dad says, anyway. The Turk hates *negros* and Metsicans."

"He made Betty sit on a curb the night we went to the Legion," I told him. I let myself think: He *is* a mean son-of-a-bitch, and it felt okay to hear myself say that.

I wasn't allowed to go to Lawrence's funeral either, but Little went. He told me Big picked him up in their dad's car, and they skipped school and went together. He said the service was real long. Way longer than a Catholic funeral, but it didn't feel long because the choir sang real good, and the music was happy even though everybody was crying. I wish I could've gone to the funeral because I wanted to tell Melinda I was sorry about her brother. I didn't know Lawrence, but I said hi to him a couple of times when I walked Melinda home after school.

Melinda's house was about two blocks from the Mission. It's the only one I know besides Betty's that has a fireplace and the only two-story house in Sangra. One time I asked her if she liked living upstairs. I told her about the club and how much fun it was that everything looked different from up there, and I asked her if living upstairs was fun. She told me that it was a little bit fun but mostly it was a bother going up and down stairs all the time. And she said they never lit the fireplace "but for New Year's Eve." I liked how she said, "but for New Year's Eve."

Anyway, Little said the choir sounded like those rhythm and blues singers his sister Marta listens to on the *negro* radio station. He said the church was packed with *negros*, but that some Mexican boys who were on the frosh football team with Lawrence were there too. He said Melinda sat in the front row crying real hard, and her dad was hugging her tight. He thought she looked back at him so he waved at her, but he guessed she didn't see him because she didn't wave back. After, there was a funeral procession in cars to the graveyard, but Big and him didn't go because Big's mom didn't want them to take his dad's car to the *tinto* part of Pasadena.

It took me two whole weeks staying in at recess and after school to catch up with my work because of all the days I was missing. One of those days was to go with Dad and Grandma to court in downtown L.A. for Rudy's parole violation hearing. Dad woke me up around 5 am so I could shower the pee off me before we left.

I fell back asleep when the car started. When Dad woke me up, we were in a parking lot near the *placita* on L.A.'s Main Street. Grandma told me we were going to go to 6:30 Mass before Rudy's hearing. After Mass, we had our breakfast tacos on a bench in the *placita*.

After City Hall, the Hall of Justice is the biggest building downtown. Inside, white men in wrinkled brown suits walked around carrying brown briefcases. Grandma wore a nice dark dress and dark sweater and her hat and the black gloves she always wears to Mass. Dad was wearing suit pants and a sport shirt and his good sport coat. I was dressed like Dad.

The hearing was on the fifth floor, and the courtroom was big and cold and almost empty. When we walked in, a white policeman and a white lady were smiling and talking at a side desk, but when they saw us they put their smiles away. Dad sat us in the back row.

In a minute, another white man in a wrinkled suit rushed in. He took a fast look at us then stopped at the cop and the lady, said something to them, and disappeared through a side door. In a minute the man came back out and put his brown briefcase on a table near the cop. He took out some papers, looked at them then put them back in his case.

The side door opened again. Another cop came out leading Rudy. His face still had bruises, but his black eyes were gone. The cop led him to the table next to the man in the wrinkled suit.

Rudy was wearing dark blue overalls and was handcuffed behind his back. Before he sat down, he looked up and saw us.

His face changed a couple of times in a few seconds—first his eyes got real big, then his face brightened and he almost smiled. But real quick his eyes filled with tears. Then he looked down and away.

Grandma started sobbing. Dad put his arm around her. She took a handkerchief out of her purse and put it to her mouth.

A loud voice said, "All rise." A door opened and a judge in a black robe came in and sat at his desk. When he sat down, everybody else sat down too.

The judge said something and the wrinkled man and Rudy stood back up. The judge said something else. Rudy's shoulders sagged like somebody pushed them down. Then the judge nodded his head, and the wrinkled man turned around and nodded to us. Rudy turned around to us, and the cop moved closer to him.

Dad got up, then Grandma, so I stood up too. Dad led Grandma up to where a short wall separated us from Rudy, and Rudy moved so that he was just on the other side. Grandma threw her arms around his neck and now she was crying real loud like she did at Grandpa's funeral. Dad tried to pull her arms away, but it was no use. She wouldn't let go.

Rudy let her do it. He kept saying, "*Tranquila, 'ama. Yo me cuidaré.* I promise, *'ama.* I'll be all right."

Grandma finally let go and made the sign of the Cross on his forehead and chest a bunch of times like she does to me when she tucks me in at night.

When Grandma finally let go of Rudy, Dad nodded his head, and Rudy nodded back. I thought Dad was going to hug his brother, but he just stood there looking down at his hands until Grandma moved me closer to Rudy. I got next to the wall and put my hand on Rudy's arm. It felt skinny and weak, like a dead tree branch. I slid my hand down his arm and bumped into the handcuffs. The metal was heavy and cold.

Rudy smiled at me, but I knew he didn't mean it. His eyes were filled with tears. "When are you coming home again?" I asked him. I felt stupid as soon as I said that. It sounded like he was just visiting us. Now that I think about it, he was.

"Promise me you'll write to me, Man-on-Fire. I'm going to miss you." The way he said my name hurt my heart.

"Time." The guard said it low in Rudy's ear. Rudy turned and started walking toward the door he came in. Grandma started crying again, and I thought of how she told me a long time ago that the Blessed Mother's heart was wounded seven times by what they did to her son Jesus.

I wondered how many wounds Grandma had.

We ate lunch at Phillipe's near Olvera Street. That should have been a big deal, but I had a hard time tasting my French dip or the Coke Dad bought me. The sandwich tasted like paper and the soda tasted like fizzy water. All I could think of was the brown bus.

After we got out of court, Dad drove the car around the block to another side of the Hall of Justice. He didn't want to, but Grandma made him.

"'*Amá*, the sooner we leave downtown, the sooner you'll get over your pain."

Grandma folded her arms and turned away from Dad. "What do you know about my pain?" she mumbled out the side window.

We waited until a gate opened and a brown bus with "Los Angeles County Sheriff" on the side in big gold letters and bars on the windows came out of the bottom of the building. The bus stopped at the street then made a right turn and disappeared into the downtown traffic.

Six more years. That's what Dad said the judge gave Rudy. Six plus the three he still owed from the last time. Nine years. Arithmetic is my favorite subject, but I didn't like these numbers. I'd be twenty-one when he came home again unless he got another parole. By the time he came home for good I might be in the army like Dad. Or the Marines. Or maybe just working. I would be a man, and Rudy would be old.

When he was home, I always wanted to play catch with him out in Main Street, but we never got the chance. And he told me once he wanted to take me fishing in the San Gabriel Canyon. I never fished before. I still haven't. Now I was going to have to wait for Rudy to take me. Or me take him.

I looked at my sandwich there on the plate. I only took two bites. My Coke bottle was mostly full.

"We have to go," Dad said. "I can still get in half a day at work." He put the last piece of his sandwich in his mouth and stood up.

Grandma took my sandwich and folded it in waxed paper. She still had most of her sandwich, and she wrapped that one too. She put the sandwiches into the bag she brought our breakfast tacos in and folded the top shut. I sucked up as much of my Coke as I could through the paper straw, but I sucked too fast and the bubbles fizzed up and burned the inside of my nose.

I looked up at the sky the rest of the way home. Pretty soon our car was back in the driveway, under the ramada Grandpa built a long time ago before I was born.

For the next week Dad made me come straight home after
school and stay in the yard. Betty had to take Ted to work
so she could have the car to pick me up from school, but I never
heard neither of them complain about helping Mom and Dad
with me.

Dad called a lawyer and made me tell him about what
happened to Lawrence. Dad didn't say much about what the
lawyer said was going to happen to me, but he did say the lawyer
told him not to let me say anything to anybody else about what
I saw at the train station. I didn't tell him I already told Danny
because that was a club secret, so it didn't count. I wondered if the
other kids in my class thought I got polio or something because
I was missing so much school now. And Dad was missing work.

Another week later me and Dad drove up to the courthouse in
Pasadena to talk to a man from the District Attorney's office. Dad
said the lawyer he talked to set up a meeting for us with the D.A.

The man we met was a deputy D.A. The word deputy made me think of cowboy movies where the sheriff has a sidekick who wears a badge, but this man was dressed in a suit. He was a tall, skinny old-looking white man who looked like it hurt him to move. He had long, bony arms and legs, and he made faces when he talked. He shook a bony, white hand with Dad and then me, and he said his name was Mr. Fullmer, and he asked me my name.

I watched his eyes follow the port-wine stain from my neck to my ear while I told him "Manuel Maldonado, Junior, Sir" without *a sus órdenes*. He asked me if I wanted a Coke. I looked at Dad, and he shook his head. I said, "No, thank you."

Mr. Fullmer walked us over to a leather couch and asked us to sit down. Then the deputy told me to tell him what happened to Lawrence.

This was the fourth time to tell it. The first time was to Dad and Ted and Betty. The second time was to Danny up in the club. And the third time was to the lawyer Dad called. The story was exactly the same every time. The sounds and the cold air and the smell of blood and poop and Lawrence's dead body and throwing up and running to Betty's. But this was the first time Dad heard about the Turk. He almost hit the roof.

He jumped up from the couch and stared down at me. He said why didn't I tell him it was the Turk that night at Ted and Betty's house. The deputy put up his hand to Dad to let me tell the story, but Dad only wanted to know why I didn't tell him.

The deputy told him if he interrupted again he'd have to wait outside. Dad sat back down, crossed his arms and legs and didn't say anything else. I had thought about telling him at Betty's, but I was afraid that if I told him, he would go looking for the Turk and get beat up like Rudy. Or killed like Lawrence.

The deputy wanted to know who else I told the story to and what was I doing at the train station. Did the San Gabriel police know I saw what happened? After I finished, he told me to tell him what happened two more times, but all I wanted to do was go home and sleep.

When I got to the part about running all the way to Betty's, he stopped me and went out of the room a minute. While he was gone, I looked at Dad. He looked like he was going to say something to me again, but then he changed his mind and got up and walked across the room to a window. I wasn't sorry I didn't tell him about the Turk before.

When Mr. Fullmer came back, a lady carrying a machine on a little stand was with him. The deputy pulled a chair up next to the couch, and she sat down and put the machine in front of her. She looked at the deputy. When he started talking again, she started tapping keys on the machine. Mr. Fullmer told me to say my name again and to tell the story one more time. That would make seven times telling about Lawrence Collison dying, and I didn't want to tell it again. The deputy said I only had to tell it one more time then he would take me up to the top floor and buy me lunch.

I was the only kid in the top-floor cafeteria. There was a couple of cops eating lunch up there but none of them asked me why I wasn't in school. The food was way better than the school cafeteria. This one had green salads and jello in different colors and sandwiches and mashed potatoes and meat loaf and slices of pie and cake. I picked a tuna sandwich even though it wasn't Friday because I love tuna, and a bowl of chicken noodle soup with saltine crackers and a slice of chocolate cake. I wanted a

Coke but Coke doesn't go with chocolate cake so I decided to have a glass of milk even though milk doesn't go with tuna.

Dad had a roast beef sandwich and a cup of coffee. Mr. Fullmer just got a cup of coffee and the lady at the cash register wrote it all down on a tab for Mr. Fullmer like at Silverman's. We took our food trays to a table next to a window facing the mountains. As soon as I sat down, I looked out the window for the broken-hearted mountain like I always do. Even though I spotted the TV towers on top of Mount Wilson, I couldn't find the heart with the arrow through it. Then I remembered what Rudy said about looking at it from a different angle.

From this angle the mountains went almost straight up. There were trees and power lines I never saw from home. I looked down the mountain range and the slope was like an ocean wave ready to break on Pasadena and Monrovia and Azusa where some of my cousins live and all the way east to where the mountains disappeared in the brown air.

The tuna sandwich wasn't as good as Grandma makes and the soup was too salty to finish, but I ate all the cake and drank most of my milk before Dad said we had to go. The deputy stood up and said I'd probably have to come back in again but not to count on getting another free lunch.

Then he smiled for the first time all day and his teeth were crooked and gray so I guess he was joking about no lunch.

When we got home, I heard piano music coming from Grandpa's garage. It was a song I heard a bunch of times but played in a way I never heard before. I went inside the garage and was surprised to find Brody sitting at Cruz' piano. I already told you Brody's the *negro* who sings the bass parts in the Tones.

His real name is Marcus Brody and he lives in Monrovia and his brother drops him off at Grandma's after school on the Tones' practice days. Sometimes Brody's grandma Willie comes with Brody to massage my grandma's arms and hands.

Grandma's arthritis hurts her real bad. Dad heard about Willie that she's real good at making old people feel better, so he brought her from Monrovia to massage Grandma. At first Grandma didn't want a massage—not because Willie was a *negra* or anything, but because Grandma said massages are for rich people. But then Dad made her try it, and she liked it. Now she knows why rich people like to get massages.

When I know Willie's there, I like to go in the house and watch. When she's finished with Grandma, she gives me a little massage. Willie's fingers are bony and strong. You wouldn't think a tiny old lady could have strong fingers like that, but Willie does. One time she told me she was born in Mississippi, but then she moved to New Orleans, then Texas—like the Collisons—then to Monrovia where she got a job as a maid for a rich white family in Pasadena.

I asked her if she knew the Collison family, but she said she reckoned she didn't. I didn't care because it felt good when she rubbed my head and then my neck and then the middle of my back with her strong, bony fingers. Her hands were cool and dry. On my neck her finger skin felt like she was wearing soft leather gloves. I liked how her fingers would work the knots in my shoulder wings that gave me shivers. That made her laugh.

She told me Jim Crow chased her to California and the Lord willing he wouldn't come here looking for her. I asked her who's Jim Crow and why was he chasing her, but she just laughed again and told me to hush and made me shiver.

I figure all *negros* know each other, so when I saw Brody I wanted to tell him about Lawrence and the deputy and how the law was going to make the Turk pay, but I kept my mouth shut like the lawyer said to. I stood next to the piano and listened to Brody sing.

Negro voices are different than Mexicans'. Mexican voices like Cruz' and Rafa's can sing the same notes, but *negro* voices come from a different place that Mexican voices never been to. Brody's voice was like dark honey.

Anyway, Brody looked at me while he was singing, and I got a shiver when I saw his eyes. It scared me that he looked like Lawrence. I imagined Lawrence sitting there playing the piano. Something in my face must've been wrong because when Brody finished his song he looked behind him and he said to me, "Man, you look like you just seen a ghost." I pretended to laugh.

"Where you been, Man?" That was Cruz. I didn't hear him come in the garage. "I never see you out in the yard anymore. You miss as much school as Brody."

Brody laughed real loud and deep and honey-like. "Well, sheee-it," Brody said, "maybe we just too damn good-lookin' for school. What you say, Man? Am I right?" His smile uncovered the whitest teeth I ever saw. I shook my head yes.

"He had to go to court for killing a hobo," Cruz told Brody. "The other kids in his gang skated because Stupid here took the fall." Cruz and Big and Rafa laughed, but Brody didn't. He looked at me kind of sad.

"You shouldn't've took the fall, Man. Friends like that ain't worth it."

I didn't like the joke on me, and I didn't know what Cruz meant by skating or taking the fall, but I didn't say anything.

It made it easier to keep the truth a secret. I know none of the gang told anybody about the hobo. It must've been Marco's mom or some *metiche mitotera* in the neighborhood who saw what happened on the rightaway and had to tell the whole world.

Cruz didn't let it go. "Maybe he'll get life and be with his jailbird uncle Rudy."

Big said, "Yeah, I bet he gets the gas chamber," then he raised his leg and ripped a fart and the other guys in the group all cracked up.

I wanted to cry, but I wasn't going to give them the satisfaction. I don't know why I even went in the garage in the first place. I should've knew that was going to happen because Cruz always turns everything into a mean joke on me.

(23)

I had to go to the Hall of Justice one more time. This time Mom took off from work to come with me and Dad. Mr. Fullmer met us in an office on the second floor wearing a nicer suit than the first time. He looked like he got a haircut and a new leather case.

He sat me on another couch and told me I had to tell my story again—this time to the grand jury. He kept saying "your story," but I didn't want him to call it my story. It was Lawrence's story. He told me to tell the truth and not leave out anything. He asked me if I wanted to go over my story again, but I shook my head. I didn't need to practice. I'll never forget what the Turk did to Lawrence that night.

The phone on the deputy's desk rang, and he answered it. He told Dad and Mom that they could wait for us up in the cafeteria. Then we all got up, and he put his hand on my back and gave me a little push toward the door.

I thought we were going to take the main elevator, but the deputy took me to a smaller one with no driver. He punched a number button and smiled down at me with that gray smile, the fake kind grownups give kids.

When we got to our floor, Mr. Fullmer took me to a small office and told me to wait there and left. The place was real quiet. I couldn't look for my mountain because there were no windows so I broke the quiet by making my shoes squeak on the shiny floor.

In a minute Mr. Fullmer came back and took me next door into a courtroom half the size of Rudy's. There was no judge's chair, but there was a chair for me and two rows of seats filled with grownups. There was about half and half men and ladies, pure white people. The men were in suits and the ladies were dressed like for Sunday Mass. Besides them, there was a another white lady with a little typing machine sitting in a chair near the deputy and an older white lady sitting at a desk. Nobody was smiling.

The deputy walked me to a chair inside a witness box like they do on TV and pointed for me to sit down. As soon as I sat down, I looked all around for the Turk. The deputy had told me he wouldn't be there, but I didn't believe him.

The deputy walked up to a stand facing the rows of people. He smiled the same elevator smile at the people in the rows and told them good morning and said his name and then told them why we were there. He read some stuff to them from the papers on the stand, then I heard the Turk's whole name for the first time. The deputy said, "Everett Earl Turkness."

It was strange to hear the Turk's name said out loud after I'd been keeping him secret for so long. It was like a big sack full of schoolbooks was lifted off my back. I looked at the people to see if anybody looked like they knew who the deputy was talking about, but nobody looked surprised or nothing.

The other thing about hearing his name was that I couldn't match the sound of that name with the Turk himself. Everett Earl Turkness sounded too nice to be the name of the man who kicked Lawrence Collison's face in at the train station.

The deputy told the people he was going to give them enough evidence to bring Turkness to trial. He pointed at me and said I was a witness to the murder of Lawrence Collison. All the people turned their heads at the same time to look at me. I didn't want to see them looking at me so I kept my eyes on the deputy. I knew some of the people were looking at my port-wine stain, but I didn't care. I only wanted them to believe the story I was going to tell them.

When he was finished talking to the people he nodded his head, and a lady at a desk stood up. She told me to hold up my right hand. She asked me if I swore to tell the truth so help me God. I didn't need God to help me, but I said yes and the deputy told me to sit down.

When the deputy told me to say my full name to the people, I finally looked at them. If they were interested that I was going to tell them Lawrence's story, they didn't show it. A couple of people had that sleepy morning look people get who didn't get enough sleep the night before. One lady yawned real wide but didn't cover her mouth like you're supposed to. A man sat with his face in his hands with his eyes closed. Another lady was looking at herself in her compact mirror and another man was reading his folded-up newspaper.

Mr. Fullmer asked me where I lived and how old I was and where I went to school and what grade. I told him, but I really wanted to tell about Lawrence and his sister Melinda and their father who worked for the SP and about *negros* who came to

California to hide from Jim Crow, but when I started, Mr. Fullmer stopped me. He came over to where I was sitting and told me to just talk about that night. He gave me a smile that was realer than his elevator smile. He asked me if I wanted a glass of water and I said, "Yes, sir."

The lady who made me swear brought me a drink in a paper cup. I took a sip and put it down on the little witness wall in front of me. It tasted bad. I should've remembered how bad the water tasted because I used the drinking fountain the time we came to see Rudy. San Gabriel water's good because it has a sweet taste—even from an outside faucet—but this water tasted like medicine.

"When you're ready, go ahead and tell your story, Manuel," Mr. Fullmer said. I wanted to tell the people it was Lawrence Collison's story, but I didn't.

I started telling them about how I'm an altar boy and sometimes I serve at Thursday night rosary and benediction. The man reading the newspaper kept reading, and the lady yawned again and blinked her eyes like to keep them open. But when I got to the train station and told about hearing noises inside, their heads all snapped up and all their eyes turned to me.

Some people started writing things in their notepads. When I stopped I could hear the scratching sounds of pencils on paper. I knew that sound. I hear it when we have to take Capone's arithmetic tests. She doesn't let us use the sliding times-tables on our pencil cases, so everybody has to times out everything on paper.

I guess my mind kind of drifted because I heard Mr. Fullmer say, "Go on, Manuel." He said my name in English like "Man-you-el." I have a cousin in Azusa who calls me "Menyo." I hate how he says my name. I almost picked up the paper cup but I remembered the taste.

Anyway, I told the story of Lawrence and the Turk to the end where I run to Betty's house, and Ted calls my dad. By now all the people were interested, and some were leaning forward like they couldn't hear me too good so I talked louder near the end. When I was finished, the deputy got up from his chair and went to the stand where he had his papers. He elevator-smiled at me and thanked me. He said now the people in the rows could ask me questions if they wanted to. Then he went back to his table and sat down. I looked at the rows of people, and all of them looked back at me.

One lady who was looking down at her composition book raised her hand like we do in school. She didn't look up until the deputy called her by a number. She was wearing a yellow dress the color of Grandma's roses and a pillbox hat to match. And a string of big white pearls that looked like they cost a lot.

"You said you heard Officer Turkness' voice and you saw him leave the train station," she said. "How did you know his voice or know who he was?"

When she asked me that and I thought about it, I felt like I was hit by an electric shock. Mr. Fullmer never asked me that question before. Maybe he didn't think of it, or it wasn't important to him. My heart started pounding so hard, I thought it was going to jump out of my chest and land on the floor. The room was quiet, and I was sure those rows of people could hear my heart.

I looked at Mr. Fullmer and his face told me he made a mistake not asking me that question before. He started to get up, then sat back down and wrote something on a paper on his table. He looked up at me and elevator-smiled.

"Just answer the question the best you know how, Manny," he said. He called me Manny. I don't know if he just made a mistake, or he wanted me to feel better, or he wanted the people in the rows to think something about me. I picked up the cup and sipped the medicine water. I didn't care how bad it tasted because my mouth was so dry that when I tried to talk my voice sounded like Dorothy's. I swallowed and watched my hand put the cup down real careful on the top of the witness wall. It kind of wobbled, and I thought it was going to tip over, but it didn't.

I said I knew it was Officer Turkness because he stopped my aunt Betty's car once and made us sit on the curb.

An old man with slicked-down white hair asked me how I could be so sure by only seeing him one time. I looked at Mr. Fullmer, but he was looking down and writing again. I looked at the cup of water. It was almost empty. I took a deep breath and looked at each of the people in the rows.

I almost laughed inside because I thought of something funny. I thought all the way back to the start of summer and playing Alamo with Danny. Then I thought about throwing fruit at the hobos. I remembered how scared we all were for the days and weeks after and how we were just waiting for the police to take us to jail. I remembered the trainman telling me and Danny we broke the law by hopping the train to Colton. And now here I was in the Hall of Justice. And for some reason I thought of that Pinocchio cartoon movie where Geppetto goes looking for Pinocchio and ends up at the bottom of the ocean inside Monstro's stomach.

The old man's voice woke me up. He said, "Answer my question, son." I looked at him. He looked old like my Grandma except his skin was chalky white, and Grandma's was brown from gardening in the sun. He had on old, thick glasses and he was wearing a suit that looked too big for him. "Yes, sir."

I took a drink and finished the water and put the cup back on the wall. I watched it wiggle, and I didn't care if it fell off. I remembered what the courtroom guard whispered to Rudy.

Time.

"I killed a hobo."

I saw the deputy's head jerk up when he heard that, like he'd fell asleep and someone shook him awake. I thought he was going to pick up a phone and call the cops to come get me.

The deputy didn't get up from his desk and there was no elevator smile.

"What are you talking about?" he barked. I wanted to cry. I wanted to pee myself so I could get out of there. I wanted somebody to belt-whip me and get it over with. I wanted the cops to come and put handcuffs on me and take me straight to prison. I wanted Rudy to be on the brown bus to tell me what to do when I got there.

I heard myself say, "Me and my gang, we killed a hobo. Marco's mom called the cops and the Turk came. He knows me and everybody in my family. He knows everybody in Sangra and we all know him. We call him 'the Turk.' He beat up my uncle and killed Lawrence and he's a mean son-of-a-bitch." I didn't care if I cussed to white people. I was going to prison anyway so it didn't matter any more. Some of the people looked at Mr. Fullmer with big eyes, but he was looking at me. He stood up, walked to his stand and ruffled through his papers like he was looking for something.

"What are you talking about, killing a hobo?" I didn't care any more what they did to me. I felt like I was free of something.

"Last summer me and my friends threw oranges and lemons at hobos riding boxcars on the tracks next to Marco's house. I guess we hit one of them because we found his body on the rightaway. We told Marco's mom, and she called the police. The Turk was the one they sent."

A man sitting on the end of the front row asked Mr. Fullmer what he knew about this. Mr. Fullmer said he would look into it.

Another man said, "Tell us about the Turk, Manuel." This man said my name in Spanish. I looked at him. He was sitting in the middle of the second row and he looked like a schoolteacher. He had on a dark blue sport coat and gray wool vest with a blue tie peeking out at the top. He was younger than the old man and had a stronger voice. All the other people turned to look at him. "Tell us what you know about him."

I looked at the deputy, but he didn't do or say anything. He just stood at his stand and stared back at me. I forgot the cup was empty and tried to take a drink. I looked for the lady who brought it to me, but she wasn't at her desk. I never even saw her leave. I put the empty cup down.

"The Turk's a San Gabriel policeman. Everybody's scared of him because he's mean. He stopped my aunt because she was driving on a white street and he made us—her—sit on the dirty street curb while he searched her car."

"No, tell us more about what you saw at the train station," the man said.

I was ashamed I made a mistake. I think the man saw that because he said, "That's all right. That information's important too. But right now tell us about the train station."

I closed my eyes. I told them it was nighttime and I was cold, but I didn't want to zip up my jacket and make noise. I said I was standing by the station door and when I looked in, I heard the Turk calling Lawrence dirty names and "nigger" and I watched him kick and kick Lawrence who was laying on the floor crying and begging the Turk to stop.

The courtroom was real quiet for a long time. My eyes were closed so I didn't know what the people were doing, but I didn't care. They made me tell this story and now I couldn't get it out of my head.

"If it was nighttime, how could you see it was the Turk in the train station?"

I opened my eyes and looked at the people because it was a new voice asking me—a lady's voice and soft. She asked me again, "How could you tell it was the Turk?"

She was wearing a gray dress and a gray hat, not rich clothes like the lady in yellow. One of her hands was on the little wooden wall in front of her. It was wearing a gray glove. "How could you tell?" I didn't know what to answer. Some people wanted to know how I knew the Turk and some wanted me to just stick to what happened in the station. I took a chance and said what I said before: "I knew his voice from when we killed the hobo. Also the time he stopped me and my aunt Betty. Oh, and then there was the time he stopped me and Danny on our way home from Silverman's."

"Tell us about the time he stopped you and Danny. Who is Danny?" Her voice sounded younger than Mom's.

"Danny's my best friend," I said. "He was with me when we killed the hobo. And last summer the Turk stopped us on our way home from Silverman's. I guess he thought we shoplifted our sodas."

"Who is Silverman?"

"That's the name of the store near my house." She said to go on so I did. I told her how the Turk asked us where we got the money to buy sodas and I answered him that Danny had got it from his uncle. I told her how he beat up my uncle Rudy and sent him back to Folsom. I knew the Turk too good.

"Go on about that night then," she told me.

I tried to think about anything I didn't say before. Then I remembered something new. When the Turk walked out he was carrying something like pliers but bigger. After all the times telling the same story, I couldn't believe I forgot the pliers.

"How were they like pliers?" the teacher-looking man asked me. I thought about his question. They had two handles and jaws like a pair of pliers but they were bigger than pliers. About as long as a baseball bat. They were like my grandpa's tree-branch cutters.

"Bolt cutters?" It was another man, but when I looked up I couldn't tell who asked me.

"I don't know what those are." I looked at Mr. Fullmer and saw him write something down. I waited for the next question, but nobody said anything. Nobody talked for a long time and I could hear pencil-scratching. Then I heard the deputy click his pen and I saw him look at the people in the rows.

He said, "If there are no more questions then..." He didn't finish his sentence. I looked at the people. Some of them were looking at Mr. Fullmer. Some were looking at me. And some were looking down and writing in their composition books.

"I think you can go then, Manuel," the deputy said. I grabbed the empty paper cup and when I stood up he said, "I need to remind you that whatever was said in this room is secret. Do not tell anyone anything about what went on here under penalty of law. Do you understand? I will talk to your father if I need you back here."

"Yes, sir." When I walked past the rows of people to leave, the lady with the gray glove put her hand on my arm and whispered, "Thank you, young man." There was nowhere to throw the paper cup so I put it in my jacket pocket and walked out of the courtroom.

Mr. Fullmer took me in the big elevator up to the cafeteria where Mom and Dad were waiting for me. Dad smiled at me and Mom put her arm around my shoulder. Her hand felt good when she squeezed my shoulder. She asked me how it went and I told her "fine." She asked me if I was hungry. I wasn't, and mostly I just wanted to get out of that building.

The traffic going home on Mission Road was bad so Dad took Valley Boulevard through Alhambra. When we got to Garfield Avenue, he pulled the car into the parking lot of The Hat. Sometimes on payday Dad brings home pastramis from The Hat. This time we sat at the picnic tables in the back. I still didn't feel like eating, and I was tired. I picked at the little pieces of meat and pickles that fell out the sides of the sandwich and the crispy edges of the bread. I wanted to sleep and my head hurt. I don't know when my headache started. All I wanted to do was go home and lay down on my bed and sleep.

Ever since Rudy went back to prison, Cruz moved back to our room at Grandma's. I didn't mind sleeping on the couch and I sure didn't like sharing the bed with Cruz anymore. I didn't like getting punched and being called Pee-Baby. I asked Mom if I could stay on the couch and I was happy when she said yes.

When we finally got home, Dorothy asked me where I went with Mom and Dad. I couldn't tell her, but she kept asking even after I told her it was hush-hush. When she asked Mom, Mom told her, "Never-you-mind. Were you a good girl for Grandma?" That shut her up.

I was asleep on the couch when Cruz got home. He shook me hard to wake me up. I thought it was morning. I was surprised that I was wearing pants and they were dry. I looked around. It was starting to get nighttime and the sky was the color of blood outside the window.

"Where you been, PBM?" he said. He calls me PBM, which stands for Pee-Baby-Manny. I ignored him. "Never mind," he said, "I know you were in court." I got real scared. If he knew where I was, pretty soon Sangra would know. Then everybody in San Gabriel—even the cops—would know.

"Well? Are they going to give you the gas chamber or life?" At first I didn't understand him. Then I figured out he thought I was in court about the hobo. I told him the jury was still out. I heard that on "Perry Mason" one time.

"You're stupid," Cruz said, then he left the room. I changed out of my court clothes and took a shower even though I knew I would have to shower again in the morning. I went back to bed and slept till morning.

Going back to school after the grand jury was weird. When I came into the schoolyard to find the gang, the whole world was staring at me. When I went by the swings, kids stopped swinging to look at me. When I walked through the schoolyard, kids stopped playing kick ball and stared at me. I felt like I was a monster because so many kids were staring.

And it wasn't like kids were staring at my port-wine stain either. When they do that, I can see their eyes move. And besides, everybody at school is already used to my port-wine stain.

I saw Danny and Little by the high school fence so I went over. In no time Cruz and his pack came to where we were. Big made a huge smile and squatted down on the other side of the fence. I asked him what he was doing and he said he wanted to see how I looked behind bars. The other guys laughed.

"I'm not going to jail," I said. "You don't know what you're talking about." I looked at Cruz. "What did you tell everybody?"

His face got red and he stopped laughing. "I didn't tell everybody anything. I'm not a rata." He looked at his friends and then smiled a phony smile. "But you know how it is, cuz," he said to me. "You tell a friend and he tells a friend and he tells a friend…"

The other guys laughed. I don't know why I keep letting Cruz chop me like that because it felt like a punch in the stomach. When I was walking away somebody said, "See you later, jailbird," and I heard laughing in back of me.

When the bell rang, we lined up. Two lines by grade. Boys and girls. The lines are by alphabet so I'm in the middle of my line, one Hernandez and two Lopezes behind Little. Danny's the last boy in our line and Marco's in the sixth grade boys' line. Every single boy in my line was looking at me. And all the girls too. I looked around and I felt my face get hot. All around me, kids were still staring at me. This time I wished they were looking at my port-wine stain.

Last Christmas on the TV news there was a story about a family from El Monte that got killed in a car crash. I remember me and Little went with Big and Cruz in Big's dad's car to see where the wreck happened at the corner of Valley and Peck Road. Me and Little went along for the ride, but Cruz and Big really wanted to see the spot for theirselves. It's like they had to see the flowers and the skid marks and the busted light pole to make the story real.

That's how it seemed to me standing in line. I guess kids heard about me—thanks to Cruz' big mouth—and now they needed to see the murderer for themselves. I looked down at the ground until the bell rang again and the parade music sent us to our classroom.

When my class was all inside, Capone started us on our morning prayer. When we finished, she said, "Children, Manuel is in class today. Let's welcome him back." Everybody turned to look at me. My face had cooled off from outside, but I could feel it getting hot again. I wondered if Capone knew what all the kids thought they knew. Then I got my answer.

"Manuel, your classmates and my sisters are praying for you and your family." She knew. "I know it's hard, but offer it up for the poor souls in Purgatory. Class, let's all say a Hail Mary for Manuel." Everybody said the prayer staring at me, then Capone walked to her desk and sat down and said, "Now we all need to concentrate on our studies. Take out your composition book and start your five-minute journal."

I lifted the lid of my desk and pulled out my journal and opened it. The date of the last time I wrote in it was just six days ago. I was surprised because it felt like I was gone a month. I sat there trying to think of what to write. I couldn't lie, and I couldn't tell the truth. I couldn't write that I didn't kill a hobo, and I couldn't write that I was a witness of a murder. I looked up at the clock at the back of the classroom. Only one minute went by. Finally I decided to write what I knew about the Southern

Pacific Railroad. I wrote that it goes from the Pacific Ocean across the U.S. to the Atlantic Ocean. By the time Capone rang her little desk bell, I wrote five pages. That was the most I ever wrote down in my journal and I don't even remember writing it.

That school week went by in a fog for me. Capone caught me daydreaming a bunch of times. She didn't say anything to me. Her fingers just squeezed my shoulder and hurt me back to work. One day at lunchtime all anybody wanted to know was when was I going to prison so I made up a date and told them, and after that everybody left me alone except for Danny and Marco and Little.

We didn't hear back from Mr. Fullmer, and that just made things worse. I couldn't think at school and I was way behind in my work. Capone made me and my mom meet with her after school.

When the bell rang at the end of the day, I stayed in my desk when everybody got up and left. They all looked back at me. I knew they thought it was about prison, but I couldn't tell them the truth.

My mom sat next to me in front of Capone's desk and Sister Alphonsus showed her all the missed work and bad test scores. Mom knew why and I knew why, but we couldn't tell Capone. All Mom could say was that that she was going to take away TV on school nights and check my work every day. What Capone didn't know was that I already didn't watch TV on school nights and Mom always checks my work. Even though things were going bad, that's one thing good: Mom wasn't mad at me about school. And if she was scared they wouldn't promote me to eighth grade next year, she didn't show it.

I stopped going up to the club until Danny and Marco and Little came to the bedroom window one day. I was laying on Cruz' bed reading a horror comic about a guy buried alive in a coffin when I heard meow and saw the three of them through the window screen. I told them to come in, but they stayed outside. It was Little who talked.

"We need to have a meeting in the club."

I didn't say anything. I just left the comic on the bed and met them at the side porch. Nobody said nothing until we got up to the club.

"When were you going to tell us what happened in the court?" Little asked me. He was laying on his back looking up at the sky.

"I don't know," I told him. "I ain't been at school and I guess I just needed some time to go by before I talked to you guys."

Marco was sitting next to me.

"My mom says you'll probably go to juvvie for a couple of years," he said. "I don't like that you're the only one that's in trouble but I'm chicken to tell the police I was there too."

Danny stared at me but stayed quiet. I sat with my knees pulled up to my chest trying to think where to start. "Nobody except Danny knows what's really going on," I said to them. "All that stuff with the court don't have nothing to do with the hobo."

I saw Marco and Little jump a little bit when they heard that. I must have talked for an hour about Lawrence and the Turk. I told them the whole story just like I did to Dad and Betty and Ted and the lawyer. Just like I did to Mr. Fullmer and the lady with the machine. And just like to the people in court.

The story was always the same except for the bolt cutters. I still couldn't think of a single thing else I ever left out. And my brain could still smell the B.O. and the poop in that dirty train station. I could see Lawrence's shiny black face and caved-in mouth. When I finished the story I looked at Marco and Little. They looked shocked. And I was glad. That meant Danny kept my secret. I wasn't surprised. I expected him to keep it. He's my best friend and that's a club rule. I was glad club rules were important to him too.

"Is the Turk going to jail?" Little asked.

"I don't know," I told him. "The deputy says they're going to go after him."

"I hope they fry that son-of-a-bitch." That was Danny.

Little sat up. "So court wasn't about the hobo?"

"Nah." Then we were all quiet for a little while.

Little said, "That means they're still going to come for us."

But Marco said, "Why would they wait so long?"

Danny said, "Maybe they forgot."

"I'm sick of waiting for the cops." Little said. It could have been me who said that. That how I felt too. We all sat in the shade in the club for a while. Then Little stood up. "I'm going home. I guess we just have to wait some more."

The other guys got up too. Marco told me, "I'm just glad you didn't go to juvvie. I wouldn't want you to be the only one." I patted him on the shoulder to say thanks.

Danny was the last one to stand up. He slapped his pants legs to shake off the stuff that falls from avocado trees. "Well, I still think they forgot about us. I'm sick of worrying about it. I'm not going to wait anymore for them to come and get me."

Grandma tells me life is one of God's mysteries, and I believe her. It was a mystery how the date I told my class I was going to prison was the date I left for prison. Two weeks after the grand jury, Grandma got a telephone call. I found out because when I got home from school Betty was at our house and Grandma was crying like I never seen her cry before. More than at Grandpa's funeral and more than when Rudy got sent back to prison.

Dorothy wanted to go to Grandma, but Ted took us to wait in the front room. Grandma's bedroom door was closed but I could still hear the awful sound of her crying. She sounded like an animal that's hurt real bad. Ted went into her room and Betty came out. She must've been crying too, because her eyes were all puffy, and her nose was red. She closed the door real quiet like when you don't want to wake somebody that's sleeping and came out to the front room. Dorothy asked Betty what was wrong. Betty sat down on the couch next to Dorothy and hugged her. She said, "Honey, we got some bad news. Uncle Rudy had a heart attack and he's real sick." She waited a few seconds. "The doctor told Grandma that it's so bad he probably won't make it."

Dorothy scrunched up her face. "Make what?"

Betty pulled Dorothy's head to her chest and started crying. When she saw me looking at her, she let go of Dorothy and wiped her eyes with a hankie. Betty told her, "He's dying."

Dorothy turned to me with big eyes "Uncle Rudy's going to die, Manny!"

Betty said to me, "Grandma's very upset, so it's better if you two stay out here until your mom and dad get home. Do you have any homework, Manny?"

"Just arithmetic and reading."

Betty told me to start my homework and to call her if I needed help. Dorothy laid down on the floor and opened her Cinderella coloring book. I stayed on the couch and took my reading book out of my bag and opened it to a story I started reading in class about a Dutch boy who saves his town from a flood. Well, I heard he saves his town but I don't know myself because I never got to the end. I was at the part where he's walking along a road by a dike and he sees water squirting out of a hole. I tried reading, but I couldn't get Rudy out of my head. I pictured him all bandaged up in the hospital like the time the Turk beat him up. I tried to understand how so much bad stuff could happen to one person. I thought about all the prayers Grandma says for Rudy and I wondered why God wasn't paying attention to her. What was she doing wrong? Or if God doesn't know Spanish. And what were all those saints supposed to be doing for her besides standing around in that glass case?

I heard my dad's car come in the driveway and the doors slam. I shut my book and saw Mom at the kitchen doorway. I looked down at Dorothy. She was asleep on the floor with her arms crossed under her head on top of her color book. Mom asked me if I was all right and I told her yeah. She went into her room and came out with a blanket and covered my sister.

"Do you know about Uncle Rudy?" she asked me. I told her Betty told us he was going to die.

Grandma's bedroom door opened and Dad came through the kitchen. He walked past Mom without looking at us and went into their room. He closed the door loud. Dorothy moved a little bit but stayed asleep. Mom went to her bedroom door. Before she went in, she said to me, "Don't bother your dad. He's upset."

I didn't know what to do. I couldn't go to Grandma's room and I couldn't bother my dad. I thought about going over Danny's and telling him the news, but I thought Dad would yell at me if he needed me for something and I wasn't there. I thought about watching TV but something told me now wasn't the time for TV. I looked at my book. I didn't care about the Dutch boy and the dike. All I cared about was Rudy.

Grandpa died after his stroke and now Rudy was dying of a heart attack. I used to think only old people like Grandpa had heart attacks, but I guess I was wrong. I wondered how a heart attack feels. How bad it hurts. If it was like how my heart hurts when Cruz is mean to me in front of other people. Or if a heart attack is really when a person does so many bad things that all his heart can do is hurt itself real bad. Or maybe a heart attack feels like there's an arrow sticking in it. I thought about Rudy being in prison again and how sad he must've been to be like a rat in a cage.

I wondered why my dad was mad. I know sometimes he's mad because he's just mad but sometimes—like when he has a fight with Mom—he looks mad, but is really just sad.

I heard my parents' voices in the bedroom. I couldn't tell what they were saying, but their voices sounded different. Usually when they fight, both their voices are loud. We can hear them all over the house. But this time, I could only hear my dad.

My mom's voice was soft and caring like it was when Dad belt-whipped me for hopping the train and she tried to make me feel better. She wasn't fighting with Dad. Dad was fighting with something else.

When the door opened only Mom came out of the bedroom. She came over to where we were and told me that Friday we would be going up north to be with Rudy. I asked her what hospital he was in and she said it was somewhere near Rudy's prison. She said we would be missing school on Friday and Monday and maybe Tuesday because the hospital was far away.

Right away I thought about how much more school I was going to miss. I didn't want to stay in seventh grade when Danny and Little would be promoted to eighth. I thought about the sixth graders in school behind me and how I only knew a couple of them besides Marco and how I'd have to make friends with younger kids. Cruz and his crowd would make fun of me for sure.

I asked Mom if I could stay with Betty and Ted but she said no, that Betty and Ted and Grandma were going with us and besides, Dad needed me to go. I didn't get why Dad needed me, but I didn't ask. While she was talking, Dad came out. He didn't look at us but went back to Grandma's room. His steps were slow and heavy, and he didn't say a word. Mom told me to leave Dad alone for now.

26

When Mom woke me up Friday morning it was still night outside. I took a quick shower while Mom took off the sheets and blankets. I'm glad Cruz wasn't there. He stayed overnight at his house, and he would stay there while we were gone.

When I got out of the bathroom Dorothy was sitting at the kitchen table. She was supposed to be eating breakfast, but she had her head down on her arms, and I knew she was asleep. I sat across from her. Grandma was dressed and at the stove making tacos like for Rudy's court day. Mom poured coffee from the pot into the thermos Dad always takes to work. Mom shook Dorothy awake and told her that if she didn't eat she wouldn't have food again until lunch. Dorothy didn't eat, so Mom threw her cereal down the drain and sent her to get dressed.

We were going in two cars. Dad and Mom and me and Dorothy would go in our car, and Ted and Betty and Grandma were going in Ted's. When Dad pulled into the street, I looked out the back window and saw Ted follow us.

We took the Ridge Route and got to Bakersfield after three in the afternoon. When we stopped for gas, I found Bakersfield on the map Mom pulled out of the glove compartment. I had put a circle around Folsom and was drawing a line with a crayon to track our trip up Highway 99. I was already tired of being in the car, and when I saw how far we still were from Folsom, I was disappointed.

We gassed up and drove through Bakersfield. When we got to the other side of town, we saw a sign that said KERN RIVER and crossed a high bridge. I stretched to see the river, but it was too far down. Dad told us that when he was a kid, almost all of Sangra would go up north to pick crops in the San Joaquin Valley. They would camp by the Kern River for a couple of days going and coming from the *pisca*. Then he was quiet for a few miles.

When he talked again, he said, "I drowned in the Kern River." Mom turned her body to face him. "What're you talking about?" Dad drove another mile before he talked again.

"I was about your age, Manuel. A bunch of us kids went swimming in the Kern. I can remember it like it was yesterday. The water was freezing cold, but we didn't care because the weather was hot. Families usually camped in the same spots every season, and somebody sometime had tied a rope to a high tree branch, and we would swing out and then let go and jump into the cold water."

Dad said that some years the Kern would run real high if it snowed a lot in the Sierras the winter before. That year the river was so high, families had to pitch camp father back from the bank. The part of the river where the rope swing was tied was quiet but more toward the middle the current was swift. Dad said he remembered swinging and jumping into the cold water and then the current got him. Before he knew it, he got pulled underwater, then let go, then pulled back under. When he came up, he could see boys running along the bank trying to keep up with the current. He could hear the boys yelling for help and yelling at him. "Swim, Manuel!"

But he couldn't swim, because the current was too strong. He felt his legs getting torn up by underwater tree branches. He swallowed a lot of water, and the cold burned his throat. He was getting tired fast so he tried to reach for tree branches or rocks or anything he could grab to stop himself. He was pulled underwater a bunch of times, and he said the roar of the water was louder than an SP train.

When he got a chance to see the bank, only Rudy and some other kid were running to keep up with him. But he couldn't do anything while the river threw his body at one boulder after another. If he didn't drown, he said, the underwater rocks were going to beat his brains out.

"At that point, I wanted to die and just get it over with, it hurt so much," he said. "But just when I was going to let go and let the river have me…" Then he stopped. He was looking out the windshield, and his head was real still. I looked out the front to see what he was staring at but there was just straight road. Mom touched his shoulder, and he kind of shivered.

"Just when I was ready to give up, something grabbed my arm. I felt my shoulder pop, and I was pulled underwater. The river wanted me, but whatever was holding my arm wanted me more. I breathed in cold water. The cold burned my lungs so bad I had to take another breath, and when I did, all I got was more freezing water."

I could see Dad's eyes in the inside mirror, and I saw them

take a quick look at me before he looked back at the highway. He said, "You know, the Kern's still a dangerous river even after they built that new dam up in the foothills, but before that it was even deadlier. The locals still call it the 'Killer Kern' because so many people drowned in it. I've heard stories about people getting swept away by the current and ending up fifteen, twenty miles downstream, all torn up from the underwater rocks and trees.

"I would've been okay dying there. My lungs were burning, and I couldn't feel my arm—I found out later that my shoulder had been dislocated. I could feel myself going away. It was like a dream and a nightmare at the same time. It felt like falling asleep in a noisy place because all of a sudden everything was dark and quiet.

"When I woke up I was in a hospital room in Bakersfield." Dad looked at me again in the mirror. "Your grandma and grandpa were there and a priest from Bakersfield. Your grandpa said the doctor told him he didn't understand why I was alive. The priest even gave me the last rites. I guess I died. My heart had stopped, but the emergency room people brought me back. They said I was lucky my brother grabbed my arm and held on.

"I didn't understand them at first. Then your grandpa told me Rudy was able to grab me and hold on until some men pulled me out."

"Rudy saved your life?" The words just busted out of my mouth.

Dad eyed me quick in the mirror. He said, "Rudy saved my life," but he didn't sound very happy about it, like a person might who's just got rescued.

For the next miles, I sat back in the back seat and made a movie out of Dad's story in my head. I don't know what the Kern

River looks like so I imagined the stream at Marrano Beach. I tried to picture everything that Dad said, but I couldn't imagine him and Rudy as kids. I knew what almost drowning felt like and that was easier. I almost drowned a couple of times last summer in the Smith Park pool when Cruz held me underwater just to make his friends laugh until I thought I was going to die. After a while I gave up trying to imagine.

Then I wondered why Dad hated Rudy so much if he was the one who saved him. I wondered if he hated him because Rudy had saved him instead of him saving Rudy.

Or maybe this. You know how Tonto is best friends with the Lone Ranger even against other Indians because the Lone Ranger saved his life? Maybe that's how Dad felt. That he had to stick with somebody he couldn't stand. Whenever Dad had to get Rudy out of a jam, Rudy could always remind Dad that he saved his life.

We got to Kingsburg after dark. Dad pulled the car into the King's Inn Motel which looked like a castle with a little drawbridge over a ditch with drooping chains on the sides and triangle flags everywhere. About ten tiny castles were lined up in a row with a parking space next to each one.

When Dad and Ted came out of the office we drove to two castles next to a sign saying YE OLDE MOATE. I didn't know what a ye olde moate was, so after Dad parked and all of us got out, me and Dorothy ran over to see it. It turned out to be just a dirty swimming pool filled with green water inside a rusty chain link fence. It had a faded blue diving board and a blue curved slide tipped over on its side. I was about to go through the gate when Mom called us to come to our castle.

The door had a coat of arms and the word GALAHAD in fancy letters. I remembered about Sir Galahad in a King Arthur story Sister Mary Thomas read last year. I told Dorothy Galahad was a pure knight King Arthur chose to look for the Holy Grail, the silver cup that held the blood of Jesus. I didn't tell Dorothy that Sister Mary Thomas said the whole thing was just a legend.

Our castle only had one bed. Mom and Dad would sleep there. I looked around for where me and Dorothy were going to sleep. My stomach growled. The last time I ate was lunch in the mountains.

I asked Mom for a taco. She told me I could eat after I took a shower. When I came out of the bathroom a few minutes later there was an open rollaway bed in the middle of the room. Mom made up the bed, and I ate my tacos. They were still a little warm in their tin foil just the way I like them. Dad said I could have the rollaway to myself, that Dorothy would sleep with them. I finished the tacos and got in bed and ran my feet across the crispy sheets looking for the cool spot. Even though I slept all afternoon, I guess I was still tired because in a minute I was asleep.

In my dream I was drowning in a river. I was being pulled away from my family. The strong current pushed my head underwater and held it there. I felt like my heart was going to explode because I couldn't breathe. I could feel sharp rocks banging against my body like somebody kicking me and my arms were getting scraped on the branches of dead trees.

Through the clear water I could see Danny and Marco and Little running alongside me reaching down to try to grab my hand. I tried to reach my hand up to them but the current kept pushing it down. I went under a bridge and saw Dad and Ted on top reaching down to me, but they were too far away to grab me.

When I couldn't hold my breath any more, I stopped fighting the current and let myself go. When I did that, I felt my body float to the top. The current slowed down like it wanted me to just give up, and when I did it set me free. The water wasn't cold any more. It was warm, and only my legs and back were wet. I felt somebody's hand on my arm, and I knew I was safe. Or dead. The hand shook me trying to bring me back to life. It was a little hand like Marco's.

I woke up and Dorothy was standing by my bed. It was dark in the room, but I heard a small voice and I knew it was Dorothy's. "You were having bad dreams," she whispered. I sat up and looked around. I could see Mom and Dad in bed and Dad was snoring quiet-like. "You woke me up." Dorothy said.

My legs and back were still wet. The warm pee was starting to cool off and sting my legs. I told Dorothy to go back to bed, but she went over and woke up Mom and told her I peed the bed. Mom got up and put on her bathrobe. She came over to me and told me to take another shower. When I came back out in my clean *calzones*, Mom had already put fresh sheets on the rollaway.

"The rubber sheet's wet. I'll have to wash and dry it in the morning," she whispered, "but the blanket stayed dry." She held up a corner of it and the top sheet for me to get back in bed. She said, "You need to stay dry because there's no rubber sheet under you." I ran my feet across the crispy sheets looking for the warm spot. I was glad she remembered to bring the rubber sheet and ask the motel people for extra sheets.

I was afraid to go back to sleep so I spent the time thinking about Dad and Grandma and Rudy. The people at the prison told Dad Rudy's heart attack was a bad one. That he probably wasn't going to make it. I thought that maybe that was a good thing because if he got well he would still just be back in prison.

Thinking about Rudy going back to his prison cell made me remember this guy named Raimundo. He was Little's next door neighbor until he went back to Mexico last Christmas. Everybody just called him Mundo. He raised pigeons. Sometimes when I went over Little's house, we'd go next door and look at Mundo's *pichones*. He had a big coop the size of Grandma's salón made out of chicken wire. Mundo raised all kinds of pigeons of different breeds and colors. My favorites were the tumblers.

You can tell tumblers because they have these feathers on their feet that other pigeons don't, and they only fly with other tumblers. He would let his tumblers loose. We'd watch them fly real high then tumble down through the sky toward the earth. Then, just in time, they'd pull out of their tumble and fly back to their coop.

Mundo would sell regular pigeons to white boys who would take them home. When they let them loose, the birds would fly in circles, then disappear. In a little while the *pichones* would show up back at Mundo's coop. Then he would sell them to other white boys who would let them go and in another little while come back to Mundo. Until he went back to Mexico he never ran out of pigeons or white boys to sell them to.

Anyway, those pigeons were like Rudy. Grandma would get him out of jail, and he'd be okay for a while but he'd always end up back there in his coop. I guess that's what Dad was so mad about. That Rudy didn't care what Grandma and the family did for him or what he did to us. To Rudy, the Folsom coop was his real home.

But that's not the Rudy I knew in the time we had together. Rudy treated me good. He cared about me and wanted me to grow up to be a good man like Dad. He told me to stay away from lowlifes like him because they would only bring me trouble. I told him he wasn't a lowlife—he was my uncle. He would laugh a little bit and punch my shoulder and call me a "crazy little man" then remember I didn't like that name and call me a "crazy man-on-fire." He told me not to let anybody put out that fire.

I heard the water go on next door. It was probably Ted getting in the shower. Betty says he always gets up early even when he doesn't have to go to work until later. I thought about them in the castle next door. About Betty waiting for her baby and about Ted's Purple Heart and scars. Dad once told me Ted came back from the war and right away got his job at Safeway and saved his money and built a house for Betty on the empty lot Grandpa gave them for a wedding present. And about what Betty said about Ted's nightmares and smoking reefer and not going the way of Rudy and the Purple Heart. Rudy didn't have a way to show the war hurt him bad too.

I wished the government could make a medal for men like Rudy. It'd be called the Broken Heart and they would give it to all those men who came home from war all messed up inside and not able to fit back in.

I thought about school. I wasn't sad or mad any more about how far behind I was. In a way, I felt like the things that were happening to me like killing the hobo and seeing the Turk kill Lawrence and going to court and now going to see Rudy in the hospital again were like that time me and Danny got stuck on the train and taken to Colton. The things that happened were carrying me along. I couldn't control where they were taking me. It was like that river dream I just had. The current was too strong to swim out of. The only thing I could do was just let go and hope somebody would grab me and save me before I drowned.

The sun came in through a gap in the window curtains and flashed in my eyes. I moved my head back into the shadows and decided that staying in seventh grade wasn't so bad. I would be in the same grade as Marco. I could still have Danny and Little one more year before they were on the other side of the high school fence from me. And we could still have the club.

The room was getting more light. I got up to close the gap in the curtains. Now I could see Mom and Dad and Dorothy on the bed. Mom was facing the window and Dad had his arm around her. He was still giving out a quiet snore. Dorothy was asleep closest to me. She was on her back and her brown curls covered her pillow like spilled coffee. She was holding her stuffed giraffe tight against her face like she always does when she sleeps. That poor giraffe's neck got broken a long time ago and now it won't stand on its own because the head flops and tips it over.

The sound of water stopped next door. In a little while Mom would get up. She was always up first at home because she took longer to get ready for work than Dad. Dorothy would be the last one up. I looked at Dorothy again. She doesn't wet her bed like me. I hope she doesn't have my kind of dreams either.

We were finishing breakfast in a coffee shop in Fresno. I was looking at my map to see how far we still had to go to get to Folsom. Ted was out at the pay phone by the bathrooms talking to the hospital. There was still half of two pancakes left on my plate, but I was full. I looked at Mom and she shook her head to tell me not to try to clean my plate.

Ted hung up and signaled with his chin for Dad to go outside with him. I could see them through the front window standing between our two cars talking. Dad slumped against the fender of our car and Ted put his hand on his shoulder. They stayed that way a long minute. Then they walked back in. Dad told Mom to take me and Dorothy back to the car. I pushed my plate of half-pancakes away and folded up my map and scooted out of the booth.

Everybody else stayed inside. We could see them from the car. Betty was sitting next to Grandma, but Dad and Ted were standing up. Grandma had her back to the window. Then her body went all stiff, like somebody made her sit up like Capone makes me. She must have screamed because all the people I could see through the front window turned their heads real fast and looked at our table.

Dad put his hand on her shoulder, but Grandma pushed it away. Then Grandma disappeared. I mean one minute she was sitting next to Betty and the next minute Betty was by herself. Then Dad and Betty leaned over and tried to lift Grandma up. I seen people faint in movies. I always thought it was fake, but I guess Grandma fainted and now Dad and Betty were having a hard time trying to get her up.

A white waitress ran back to the counter and brought a glass of water. A white man from another table came over, but Ted shook his head and said something and the man patted his shoulder and walked back to his booth.

They finally got Grandma to sit up. Dad slid into the booth beside her. I wanted to go back in and be with them. I pushed Dad's seat against the steering wheel so I could get out of the backseat, but Mom turned back to look at me.

"Where do you think you're going?"

"I just want to help Grandma."

"Then help her by staying still. Fix the seat and stay put."

Grandma's shoulders were jumping up and down. I knew she was crying real hard. Then little by little Grandma's shoulders calmed down. Dad give her a kiss on the forehead and slid out of the booth. He came back out to the car. He looked older than he did before we went in that coffee shop.

"Rudy's gone," he told Mom.

"Where?" Dorothy asked Dad.

"Rudy's dead."

"No!" I yelled.

"The hospital told Ted Rudy must've had another heart attack. They said they checked on him at four this morning, but when they checked again at six he had no pulse. They said they tried to bring him back, but they couldn't."

We all got quiet in that car. Mom lifted her arm over the back of Dad's seat. She whispered "I'm so sorry, Manuel," and touched the back of his neck the way she does to me when she kisses me goodnight. When Mom touches me like that it tickles and makes me shiver, but Dad stared straight ahead like he didn't even feel a thing.

"We're going home," he finally said. "Ted's going on to Folsom so Mother can claim Rudy. They'll put him on a train and send him home. We decided I should go back to make arrangements at Bouchard's." Dad's voice was hard and sharp and heavy.

I wanted to ask him if I could go with Grandma, but I decided to keep my mouth shut. I looked at Dorothy who was squeezing Giraffe. She was crying without making any sounds. Big tears were rolling down her cheeks making Giraffe's spots darker. Mom moved over next to Dad and put her head on his shoulder. I knew she was crying. I wanted to cry too, but more than that, I wanted to be like Dad and he wasn't crying.

It was real late at night when Dad pulled the Chevy under the ramada. The drive from Fresno took all day and nobody talked the whole way. We stopped in Bakersfield again to gas up. I didn't even taste the cold tacos I had to eat for lunch. I didn't care about places on the map because all I could think about was Rudy laying there dead in the hospital.

I remembered when Grandpa went in the hospital after his stroke. Dorothy was a baby, and Mom didn't let me go visit him. I think he was there only three days before he died, but I remember how sad and empty the house felt when he was gone. I hardly saw Grandma those three days and when I did she looked so sad and old.

I think the worst part was Grandpa's *velorio*. There were lots of people at the Mission for the rosary the night before his funeral. The coffin was open, and it seemed like everybody from Sangra got in line to see Grandpa off.

At first his old friends went by. Old ladies blessed him. Old men stood with their Mexican cowboy hats in their hands or leaned on their wood canes. So many people hugged Grandma. I didn't know anybody could cry as many tears as she did when her friends put their arms around her. The men gave respectful *abrazos* to my dad and mom and Betty and shook hands with Ted and touched my shoulder with their rough old hands.

After everybody else left and the Mission was almost empty, Dad and Mom helped Grandma walk to the coffin to say goodbye to Grandpa one last time. Betty held my hand and we walked behind them. I didn't want to look at Grandpa. I was scared of what he was going to look like. Betty had to pull me up to make me walk with her. I pulled back, but she glared at me and shook her head.

At the coffin I stood between Dad and Ted. I didn't want to look down at Grandpa. I wanted to close my eyes and just picture him the way I always saw him in his blue overalls and Mexican cowboy hat watering his plants or cutting branches off bushes or sweeping the driveway with the big push broom he used just for that job. I wanted to imagine him sitting at the kitchen table eating *cocido* with a spoon in one hand and a rolled-up tortilla in the other. I wanted to see him fixing my kite after I broke it trying to pull it off the telephone wires on the rightaway.

Dad tapped my shoulder. I opened my eyes and looked down. I thought I was going to see Grandpa but instead what I saw was a statue of Grandpa wearing the blue wool suit he always wore to Sunday Mass. The statue's waxy white hands were crossed and holding a blue rosary. I never saw that rosary before. Grandpa never said the rosary with me and Grandma. I don't know where they got that rosary to put in the statue's hands.

I looked at the statue's face. It didn't look like Grandpa. Grandpa's face was always sunburned up to his white forehead where his cowboy hat stopped because Grandpa was always outside tending his garden, but this statue was white like a candle and the skin was pulled tight like a bed sheet to get rid of the wrinkles. And it was smaller than Grandpa. The suit fit it big like my suit fit me before Mom took it apart and sized it to my body. The longer I looked at the statue the gladder I was that Grandpa wasn't there.

The inside of the coffin was real fancy the way they made the sateen wrap around the statue in a million little pleats. And all around were pictures and holy cards and roses and other things people put inside when they said goodbye. I felt Dad next to me shaking. I looked up. He wasn't crying, but his body was shaking and his eyes were closed. I took his hand with mine. It was rough and hard. He wrapped his hand around mine and squeezed it for a long time. His shaking arm made my whole body shake until he let go and turned me away from the coffin by my shoulder.

We walked down the aisle of the Mission church. I looked back one last time before we went outside. I saw Mr. Bouchard close the lid of the coffin with Grandpa's statue inside.

♐

Grandma's house was dark and cold. I didn't sleep the whole way back because I wanted to stay awake to help Dad stay awake. I heard stories about people falling asleep behind the wheel and going off the road, but Dad was careful and got us home safe. Dorothy was asleep choking Giraffe and Mom fell asleep around San Fernando, but she woke up when Dad turned off the car.

I went straight to my old room. I wanted to get under the blankets because I was real tired now but Mom told me to wait until she made the bed and put on the rubber sheet, so I just sat on the front room couch and waited. I was glad Cruz wasn't there. Dad came in carrying Dorothy and put her in the bed in their room. Mom came out of my room at the same time Dad came out of theirs. She put her hand on his shoulder.

"Don't stay up too long. You really need to sleep." Dad didn't say anything. He just went out the front doors and closed them behind him.

Mom didn't have to tell me to go to bed. I went in my room and got undressed. It was weird laying there in bed all alone without Cruz. The light of a full moon came in through the blinds so I had to turn my back to the window to face the dark side of the room. I heard a night train coming on a west current. That must be the train that always starts my nightmares and makes me pee myself. But this time I was already awake.

The train got louder as it got closer. The horn blew four times, and the house rumbled and shook when the locomotive went by. This time that train wasn't scary at all. This time it wasn't an angry monster, not a black snake spitting sparks and smashing houses. This time it was just a train like all the other ones I saw and felt go past our house minding their own business and getting where they needed to go.

After the engine passed, the boxcar wheels clickity-clacked over the joints of the rails. The horn warned when the engine was about to cross Del Mar and again, lower and quieter, when it was near the Mission. Every now and then the clickety-clack broke and I could just hear the tick-tick-tick from the steel wheels.

Pretty soon the train sounds died away. But the night wasn't quiet.

There was a choking sound, maybe a dog pulling against a chain, but it was closer than Cerberus. It was coming right from the front porch. I got out of bed and snuck to the front window and split open the venetian blinds.

Dad was sitting in the hobo chair. His shoulders from the back were jumping up and down almost like they do when he's laughing at something real funny. I stayed looking out the window until he got up. I heard the screen door open and then the front door. I jumped back in bed and pretended I was sleeping.

The bedroom door opened and the floor squeaked when Dad came to my bed. He stood there for so long I almost opened my eyes to see what he was doing. Then I felt his rough thumb bless my forehead and his two-day beard scrape my cheek when he kissed it. It felt wet.

It was a long time since he said good night to me like that. That's the last thing I remember before I fell asleep.

$$28$$

When I woke up on Sunday, my bed was still dry. I turned to tell Cruz, then remembered he wasn't there. This is probably the one time I wished he was there, so I could see the look on his face.

The sun was real bright in the room so I knew I slept late. I got up and got dressed. I didn't need to put on the spare *calzones* my mom left for me on the chester drawers. Nobody was in the front room. I could hear Mom and Dorothy talking in their bedroom. I went in.

"Where's Dad?"

"He went over to Bouchard's to see about Rudy's funeral. Did you take off your sheets?"

"I don't need to. I didn't wet."

Mom tilted her head like she didn't get what I said.

"Well, that's good news," she said.

"Are we going to church?" I asked her.

"No, the last Mass is in fifteen minutes, and we won't be ready. We're all pretty tired. And besides, your Dad has the car."

I was happy and disappointed at the same time. Happy because I didn't have to get all dressed up for church, but disappointed because I would have to confess to Father Simon about missing Sunday Mass and because I knew I needed to pray for Rudy.

Grandma and Betty and Ted got in early Tuesday morning but it took another week for Rudy's body to come home on the train. Mr. Bouchard and his sons would meet Rudy's train in Alhambra and take him to their funeral home. Rudy's wake was going to be on a Friday night and his funeral Saturday morning. Dad asked me to get the altar boys for the services.

I asked Little if he would serve. He said that'd be good. None of the other guys in the club were altar boys except me and Little, but I didn't want to serve so I asked a white kid in my class named Billy Hartman to. He said okay.

Rudy's velorio was like Grandpa's in some ways but different in others. It was in the old Mission church like Grandpa's, but way less people came. There was a couple of old-timers, but most of the people were Mom and Dad's age. Father Mosqueda—who everybody calls *Mosca* because of his hunched back and black cassock and who always acts like he has someplace better to be—said the rosary in Spanish. He talked about hell a lot which I don't think he should've because everybody knew Rudy was a sinner and *Mosca* didn't have to rub it in.

When it was time for viewing Rudy's body, people lined up for one last look. Most of the people were from Sangra except for one or two strangers. I was glad the tecatos didn't show up. The people walked past the open coffin, then came over and shook Dad's hand or mumbled something to Grandma. They did that elevator smile to me and turned and left.

Danny and Marco and Little came with their families and

walked up to Rudy's coffin together. They came to me and shook my hand without saying anything. Their moms and dads shook hands with Dad and patted Grandma's hand.

When everybody was gone, it was our time to say goodbye to Rudy. I wasn't afraid this time like with Grandpa. I thought I knew what Rudy was going to look like but when I saw his face in the coffin he looked different than I remember. The last time I saw him was about two months ago, but now he looked way older and skinnier than Dad in a cheap suit that fit him way too big. And he was littler than I remember.

I looked at his crossed hands. They were almost as small as Dorothy's but bluish and waxy-looking. They were holding a rosary of black beads that were as shiny as his skin. The funeral people didn't bother covering up Rudy's faded cross tattoo on his right hand at the place where his pointer finger and his thumb split up. I knew he had other tattoos because I saw some of them when he was living with us. I remember he got one a few days before I went to the Legion with Betty. It was a little heart with the word *Madre* in a banner on his chest over his own heart. But the cross on his hand looked faded and old. He must've got it a long time ago. Maybe when he was twelve like me. I looked at that place on my hand. I know my dad would blow up if I ever did that.

I looked one last time at Rudy's face and I wish I would've spent more time asking him questions like why did he do all the things he did. I know he would've told me the truth. I just know it. Because he respected me even if I was a kid. Like Betty respects me.

When I said goodbye to Rudy for the last time, I reached in the coffin and touched the back of his hand. It felt hard and cold and I was glad, because that meant he wasn't there no more. He wasn't going back to prison. He wouldn't have to sneak around anymore and worry about messing up or cops hassling him. He wouldn't have to be sorry for doing something he knew he was going to do again. He wouldn't ever hurt Grandma again or make Dad ashamed of him or mad ever again.

And when I thought about these things I was happy for him.

When we got to church on Saturday, the funeral car from Bouchard's was already in front of the Mission. The two Bouchard sons opened the back door and slid Rudy's coffin out and set it on a table with wheels. Then six men wearing white gloves walked over and stood around the coffin. One of them was Ted. I recognized Elvira's dad and Germán and other Sangra men who I don't know their names.

Mosca came out of the Mission wearing a black cope and Little and Billy Hartman came out right behind him in their black cassocks and white surplices. I looked down at Little's feet. It was Saturday but he was wearing his shiny Sunday shoes. He was carrying the big procession cross and Billy was holding the holy water bucket *Mosca* would use to bless Rudy's coffin. Billy smiled at me, but Little looked at me with sad eyes. After *Mosca* said some prayers and sprinkled the coffin with holy water we all walked into the church. It took my eyes a little while to get used to the dark. When they did I saw that there was more people than at the velorio but still less people than at Grandpa's funeral. I walked in holding Betty's hand. Mom and Dad were in front of us with Dorothy and Grandma.

I tried to look straight ahead, but I also tried to look at who was there out of the corners of my eyes. At the back of the church I saw Big and his dad who finally got back from Mexico. Farther up I saw Danny and Marco with their parents. When Danny saw me see him he gave me that little high-sign with his chin, but I didn't give it back. Near the middle of the church I saw Cruz and a guy named Lencho who he started hanging around with at school. They were chewing gum and looking around—probably for girls.

After Mass we all walked to the Mission graveyard where they buried Rudy in a grave right next to Grandpa. We were the last to leave the cemetery. Grandma just couldn't say goodbye. Two Mexican workmen stood in the shade of a tree holding their hats and their shovels, waiting for us to leave so they could finish their job. Grandma sat by the hole in the ground and cried and dropped one flower after another into it. Finally Dad and Ted had to pick her up and make her walk away.

The funeral reception was at Dead Man's Hall. When we got there people were already eating or in line to be served rice and beans and tortillas and barbequed meat *del hoyo*. The real name of Dead Man's Hall is *Salón de la Sociedad Funeraria de San Gabriel*. The *Sociedad* is kind of a club people join to make sure their funeral gets paid for. When Grandpa died, the *Sociedad* paid for his funeral. Dad said Grandma used her *Sociedad* money on Rudy's.

Grandma didn't stay at the hall long, just enough to thank people and let them give her advice about how to feel about Rudy dying. And lots of people did. Some of them said that he was in peace now. But other people said stupid things like "Now you don't have to worry about him no more" and stuff like that.

I looked around at all the people sitting at the long tables laughing and eating, and I wondered how they could be so happy at a time like this. Some of those people weren't even at the velorio or the funeral.

I found Danny and Marco and Little at the soda tina. Danny fished a Coke out of the tub and opened the bottle for me. The soda was ice cold and tasted good, but I didn't feel like eating or listening to the happy chatter. I was getting hot in my wool suit, and the electric fans were only pushing hot air around.

"You want to go out back?" Little asked me.

"Yeah."

An alley runs behind Dead Man's Hall on the edge of the Rubio wash. We took our Cokes and went over to the fence. Danny spat a loogie. We watched it hit the little stream of water in the middle of the wash. We drank our sodas without saying anything. It felt like all of us wanted to say something but nobody did. I wanted to say thanks for coming to the funeral, but I knew they knew I was glad they came. I think they wanted to say they were sorry Rudy died in prison and not at home but I think they knew I knew that too. So we just stood there until our bottles were empty.

Marco was the first one to talk. "You going to school Monday?"

"Yeah."

"You wanna walk with us?" Danny asked. Betty had been taking me to school since what happened to Lawrence. But maybe it was time.

"I'll ask my dad," I told Danny.

"I'll be by for you at 7:15." And then we shook hands like men do. His hand was wet and cool from the Coke bottle. It felt good in my hand. Then Little followed, then Marco until I was alone in the alley.

I looked down at the wash again and watched a little piece of cardboard come down the stream spinning and snagging on the dry edge, then getting away and floating farther downstream. I watched that piece of cardboard until I lost it in the shadows of the SP trestle. I thought about Rudy and the story he told me about the war, and I wondered if that guy *Frijol* was waiting for Rudy in heaven. I wondered when Rudy saw him if *Frijol* would look okay where his head was caved in by the truck. I hoped *Frijol* would shake Rudy's hand and thank him for stopping his pain and forgive him for what he did.

I jumped when I felt a hand on my shoulder. When I turned around Dad was looking at me. He looked a little drunk. I was glad it was him.

He asked me, "Are you okay, Son?"

I looked at my empty Coke bottle. "Yeah."

"It's time to go. Come on in and say goodbye to everybody so we can go home." I nodded my head and let his hand on my shoulder lead me back inside.

I dragged myself through the week after Rudy's funeral. Nobody seemed to have much to say at the house. Grandma stayed in her room most days. It was a good thing we had lots of leftovers from the reception because Grandma didn't go near the kitchen.

Betty came over every day to check on her, but even Betty didn't feel like talking. She'd stay a little while in the afternoon to "tidy things up," and then go home without saying goodbye.

Dad and Mom would come home from work, and Mom would heat up leftovers. No one talked at dinner. The food didn't have any flavor. I left most of it on my plate anyway.

I'm glad Cruz stayed at his house because I didn't need him to remind me of anything I wanted to forget. The only good thing was that in the morning I was still waking up dry. Every morning before I had to get up and get dressed for school, I would lie in bed and try to memorize the feeling of the dry sheet under me in case it never happened again. But even with that, the days went by in black and white and gray like the shows on TV.

I walked to school with Danny and Marco. No one talked. We just stared down at the brown cement sidewalk and watched our feet take us where we had to go without saying a single thing.

One day I found a holy card on my school desk with a picture of Jesus outside his tomb. When I turned the card over, Capone had wrote a note telling me the sisters were praying for my family "in this time of your great sorrow." I looked at the date on the card. School was three weeks into October and when I looked around the classroom the bulletin boards were decorated with red and yellow and orange leaves made out of construction paper and pieces of felt.

Mostly Capone let me slide. Even though I would sit there at my desk staring at my schoolwork, I never felt her man-hand squeeze my shoulder. She didn't call on me in class—she knew I probably wasn't paying attention to the questions much less know the answers. But whenever I looked up from my desk, I would see her staring at me.

One day on our way home Danny told me he was worried I wasn't going to pass seventh grade with him so if I wanted he could tutor me after school to catch me up on everything I was behind on. I liked that idea so we agreed he'd come over after dinner, and we'd work on my front porch.

Besides, even though he gets good grades in school, it's not easy for him to study at his house with Sonia playing *negro* music loud on the radio and Rafa practicing his trumpet in the kitchen.

I don't know if Grandma's prayers finally reached God in heaven or if he finally got tired of hearing them, but on Tuesday at lunchtime when me and Danny and Marco were playing handball against the school auditorium, Little ran over and told us Cruz wanted me. I looked at the high school fence and saw Cruz waving his arm at me to come over there. Big and Cruz' other friends were around him like a king's guards.

"I don't want to talk to him." I squeezed the tennis ball in my hand. "He's just going to make jokes about Rudy."

Little looked back at Cruz, then at me. "No. He said he needs to tell you something about the Turk."

With Rudy and the funeral and all, I had forgot about the Turk. I didn't want anything to do with him, but the looks on Danny and Marco's faces told me maybe I better go talk to Cruz. I squeezed that ball all the way to the high school fence, and when I got there Cruz looked like he was ready to explode with whatever he had to tell me.

"Your uncle was lucky he barely got his ass kicked." Cruz made a stupid know-it-all smile and his followers made that same stupid smile. I didn't know what he was talking about. I was sorry I walked all that far to hear what I already knew I was going to hear.

It was Danny who answered Cruz.

"Why do you treat Manny like that, Cruz? You're mean." I looked at Danny. He was staring at Cruz the way I've seen guys do when they choose off another guy to fight. I saw Cruz' face turn red like I never seen before.

"I ain't talking to you," Cruz told him, "and besides, this doesn't have nothing to do with Rudy. It's about the Turk. Rudy's lucky he wasn't dead way before is what I'm saying."

I guess my face was a blank. Cruz must have figured I still didn't know what he was talking about.

"Just tell him, man," Big said to Cruz.

"Tell me what?"

"The Turk's in county jail and he's going to prison." Cruz looked at me to see what I was going to do next. The hair on the back of my neck stood up, but I didn't want Cruz to know how bad he shocked me.

"That's not funny, Cruz," I told him. I turned to go back to handball.

"No kidding. The sheriffs got him for killing Lawrence Collison." That turned me around. "Elvira's cousin Lino told me some guy told him the Turk copped a plea. He's going to prison."

I didn't want to believe Cruz. He lied to me so many times just to make a fool out of me. I didn't need to be fooled again. Danny and Little and Marco looked at me like they would do whatever I was going to do.

I bounced the handball on the ground. "Let's go back to our game." I felt good that this time the joke wasn't going to be on me. Cruz always knew only parts of the stories he blabbed to the whole world like the chismoso he was.

On the way home, me and Danny and Little and Marco couldn't quit talking about what Cruz said. In no time we were at Main Street and Euclid where Little had to peel off to go to his house. We could hardly wait to hear the whole story. The real story. And when one of us got it, we'd meet up in the club to share it with the gang.

I waited on the front porch all afternoon for Mom and Dad to get home from work so I could tell them what Cruz said. When Dad pulled into the driveway, I was off the porch and at his window in a flash.

"Dad. Wait till you hear what Cruz told me at school!"

Dad shut off the Chevy's motor. Mom got out of her side of the car. Dad told me to get in. He pulled out a Camel and pushed in the Chevy's cigarette lighter. He gave me a long look. When the lighter popped out, he lit his cigarette and took a big drag.

"Is it about the Turk?" he asked.

I bounced in the seat. "Yeah! Cruz told me he's in jail and headed for prison for killing Lawrence." I was expecting Dad to be excited but he took another puff of his cigarette. "What did Cruz mean when he said the Turk copped…" I couldn't remember what Cruz said.

He blew smoke out his nose. "Copped a plea? Cruz is right. I got a call at work from Mr. Fullmer last week. I didn't want to tell you until Turkness was behind bars, and you were safe. Fullmer told me Turkness' lawyer made a deal with the D.A. He agreed to admit to killing Lawrence and go to prison, but for less than if he was found guilty at trial. They agreed to a couple of years and probation."

Right away I got mad. They put people in the gas chamber for murder, but the Turk would be out of prison in no time for killing Lawrence! But Dad wasn't done.

"You can't tell anybody what I'm going to tell you, *me entiendes*? For your own protection." He sucked in and blew out another puff of smoke. "Fullmer checked on some of the things you said at the grand jury. He had the sheriffs look for the bolt cutters, and they found them in Turkness' garage. They matched them to the chain from the train station. And they matched fingerprints they found on the cutters and at the station. Your testimony sealed the deal, so the Turk took a plea."

Dad stubbed his cigarette out in the ashtray. A finger of smoke climbed up the dashboard. He turned to me and put his arm over the back of the seat like he does when Mom's in a good mood and sits right next to him.

"Mr. Fullmer called me again today at work. He said Turkness was killed yesterday." I heard every word Dad said, but it's like I couldn't understand until he said it again. "He was in a county jail holding cell waiting to be moved to Chino Prison. Some inmates got to him. Turkness is dead, Manny."

My head was spinning. I wanted the Turk to pay, but I didn't think he'd die like that. I was tired of people dying. All I wanted was for him to get punished and leave us alone. But I didn't want him dead.

"Turkness made a lot of enemies, son—a whole lot of enemies. I guess it all came back to roost for him." I thought about Mundo's pigeons coming back to their coop. "Mr. Fuller told me something else. After you talked to the grand jury, he called me at work and asked me if I knew the date you boys found the hobo on the tracks. He wanted proof to show the grand jury you were telling the truth about everything. I told him it was around the last week of June."

It seemed like it was years ago we killed the hobo, and at the same time it felt like yesterday. "He had the county coroner's check their records. They told Fullmer that a man had been stabbed. That he was all torn up from the fall off the train, but that the knife was still in him when the c-wagon picked him up. A home-made knife hobos call a "shank." They carry 'em for protection.

"You didn't kill the hobo. Somebody on that train did."

31

I ate my supper without words or taste like before, only for different reasons. And after dinner I went out by myself to the front porch. Cerberus was barking just to hear his own voice. The horn of a freight train on a west current told me it would be by soon. The night was clear and cold, but I didn't care. I stood at the little porch wall and looked way past the rightaway and the tracks and the warehouses to where the San Gabriel mountains slept like a happy black dog.

School would happen again tomorrow, and at lunchtime Cruz would tell the whole world the latest about the Turk and act like he was the first to know. But I didn't care. He could say whatever story he wanted to make up because I knew the truth. And soon Danny and Marco and Little would. If they were like me, they'd be happy we weren't going to prison but sorry how the hobo died. And they'd be glad nobody would ever again have to worry about the Turk but sad he died like he did.

It was too dark to see the broken heart, but I knew it was

there on the mountain right under the twinkling lights of the TV towers. Rudy was gone and Beans and Lawrence and the hobo and now the Turk. I never wanted any of them to die.

I knew that even though I didn't want to pray for him, when Grandma found out about the Turk she would tell me we should say a rosary for him so that God would have mercy on him for all the bad things he did to people.

And I knew she would be right.

Acknowledgments

Thank you to Linda, Emile, Bianca, Ivan, and Dante Acosta for your love, support and confidence. Thanks to Vikki Estrada Ng for your encouragement and counsel in the early development of *Iron River*. A special thank you to Rev. Ralph Berg, CMF, who launched me on my writing journey with treasured words of encouragement. Mil grácias to my collaborators at Cinco Puntos Press, especially my editor, Lee Byrd, who whipped my story into shape. Thank you to my boyhood partners-in-crime Robert Barrozo, Manuel Gonzalez, and Johnny Quiroz. RIP Manuel and Johnny.

To la gente de Sangra, I offer my great gratitude and love. Finally, if you enjoyed this story, join me in giving all praise, glory and thanks to Almighty God who allowed me to participate in this small way in his creative Spirit.

www.ironrivernovel.com

Daniel Acosta was born in Monterey Park, California and spent his childhood in San Gabriel, California, across the street from the Southern Pacific Railroad tracks. He attended Catholic seminary for four years and, afterwards, California State University, Los Angeles. Following college, Daniel was drafted into the U.S. Army during the Vietnam War. He was discharged in 1972 and returned to CSULA to earn his teaching credential and his master's degree. He taught English and creative writing at Mark Keppel High School in Alhambra, California and is a former member of the L.A. Barrio Writer's Workshop. Daniel is the father of four. He and his wife Linda live in Rosemead, California. *Iron River* is his first novel.